DEAR

Juliette

Also by Krys Marino (Merryman):

the only thing on earth (2022)

DEAR
Juliette

Krys Marino

imPRESS
Greenville

imPRESS Millennial Books
Greenville, SC

First imPRESS Millennial Books paperback edition November 2023

For information on imPRESS Millennial Books Consulting, please visit our website at www.impressmillennial.com or contact imPRESS Millennial at publisher@impressmillennial.com.

Printed in the United States of America

ISBN 9798399532493 (Paperback)

Mom,

I haven't always understood your love—
but I know it has no limits for me. I love you.

Dear Reader,

Thank you so much for taking a chance by picking up this book. I hope you can connect with at least one of these characters.

Before you start reading, I want you to be aware of a few things you'll find in this book. Although a work of fiction, this book contains the following that could be triggered from your own personal story: the death of a parent, child abandonment, the protagonist being raised by a single mother, and explicit language.

Be mindful of these real issues if you decide to continue reading and always indulge in self-care.

Krys

DEAR

Juliette

august

one

"*Jules, bonjour!* Can you hear me?" Genevieve said as she tapped my shoulder with her pointer finger, startling me awake.

I had taken a nap in one of the quiet rooms Gen was sure to find me in if she indeed couldn't locate me in my cubicle, which was conveniently placed right next to hers. I had my left arm spread out on the table, resting my left ear to it—hoping I hadn't been caught drooling, or with embarrassing red streaks across that side of my face.

Genevieve Laurent is my best friend and confidant, roommate, and coworker who I met at the Boston University College of Communication and also happens to be French-American like me. We were both in the journalism program together and happened to land jobs at B magazine, the Boston area's most elite lifestyle magazine; she became a travel writer, while

I became a food and dining writer. Nearly eight years later, we were still single as hell and living in our barely nine-hundred-square-feet two-bedroom apartment in Dorchester, which is now Boston's largest and most diverse neighborhood, but luckily, not as expensive as living in Boston proper.

She called me Jules, short for Juliette, which meant youthful, beautiful, and vivacious en français—all the things I was not feeling about myself as my thirtieth birthday neared. One, because for some odd reason people my age think thirty is the new fifty. Two, because I would never look in the mirror and say, *damn, you're hot, girl*. And three, because I felt like I was coasting along in life. I was alive, but a question I often asked myself was: Have I been living?

"What, yes, sorry. Just fitting in my mid-day power nap," I responded, sitting up and wiping my mouth in case there had been any drool lingering on the corners. I tried to fit in naps any time I could, as we were always on the run chasing stories and hardly ever got off work on time.

It didn't surprise me Gen walked into the quiet room I was in, despite the door knob-hanging sign that read: OCCUPIED. It was never like Gen to have any boundaries with me—or anyone else for that matter. But that was also a part of what made her so alluring: she is who she is, take it or leave it.

Gen is drop-dead gorgeous and wears the kind of confidence most women are envious of, but she's a kind soul. Although she is a French-American, she is mulatto. She has thick, brown hair, lightly bronzed skin, dark chocolate eyes, and plump rosy lips—without even trying, aka she doesn't need lip injections. Every time we go out I'm immediately self-conscious, because standing next to her—with my frizzy dull brown hair, I could never seem to tame, and my pale skin—what guy wouldn't choose her over me?

I was turning the big three-oh in a week, and I was a single woman living in Boston—which could be worse—working for B Magazine as a restaurant critic, which could also be worse, but I thought I would be closer to an editor title by now. My timeline was a little off, but is life ever what you think it will be? Considering my love—and obsession—with food (something my mom passed onto me) and journalism, I was working my dream job in the city I was born and raised in—I guess it's just more about the *single* part of my life that kept nagging at the depths of my biological clock.

Journalism wasn't something I fell into; it was something I knew I was destined for since elementary school. I used to watch movies like *How to Lose a Guy in 10 Days* and remember being fascinated with the profession: the research, the interviewing, the press passes and perks. So, simply put, I never stopped working toward it, nor gave up on the dream of it no matter how many times people told me it was a "dying field" and "good luck getting a job right out of college."

It took a while to get to where I am today—between working any dead-end job I could find to make rent and working freelance writing gigs. But now that I have "made it," I never take a second of it for granted. There is also no city better than Boston—in my opinion. It's clean, it's full of fun sports fans, people are wicked smaht, and the restaurant scene is *amazing*. I mean, who doesn't love a Lobstah Roll?

"Well, time's up. Listen, I know you said you didn't want to go big for your dirty thirty, but we are now a week away, and we *have* to celebrate somehow, someway...if I have any say. You see what I did there?" She grinned, knowing I had a hard time saying no to her.

As my best friend, she had a way of knowing what I wanted for myself, even at the times I didn't.

"Fine...what did you have in mind?" I asked as she smiled, gripping her bottom lip between her teeth and doing a little happy dance.

For my birthday a few years ago, Gen rented not one but two male strippers. There was no telling what was crossing her mind, but if I knew better, it would be a good time.

We hurried out of the office after work, down the elevator, through the lobby, and out the revolving door before anyone could push more work onto us. Then, we walked a short distance to the Massachusetts Avenue Station, which was a short subway ride back to our Dorchester Flats' apartment—less than two miles to be exact.

We arrived at our apartment building, not lacking any blisters from our Oxfords. When you walked through the navy blue French doors, there were two large plants on either side, mailboxes on the right, and a black and white honeycomb-tile floor. The walls were accented with shades of sand, gray, and blue paint, and watercolor paintings.

We walked to the elevator doors, and Gen impatiently hit the up button a few times. A minute or two later, we arrived on the fourth floor of the building; we could barely see all the views of the city unless we were on the rooftop. When you walked into our apartment, it was an open concept floor plan with floor-to-ceiling windows that let the natural light flood in, light oak faux vinyl wood flooring, not a single inch of carpet covered the floors, and vibrant blue accents on the doors and window framings.

I threw my laptop bag on one of the island counter stools—as I had every day—and headed to my bedroom to take a shower. There was something about going to restaurant kitchens all day for interviews that called for two-a-day showers. The mixed aromas of Asian fusion, Italian, and French cuisines, didn't mix so well together by the end of the work day. You name it, I smelled of it.

"I'm going to shower. See you in a bit!" Gen yelled out as she slipped into her bedroom.

"Sounds good. Me, too," I said as I walked toward my bedroom and closed the door behind me. I stripped my clothes off and turned the shower on, waiting for it to warm up.

After stepping inside, I let the warm water beat down on my skin, slicking my wet hair back down to my nape. I closed my eyes, wondering what crazy surprise Gen would have planned for my birthday. I wouldn't be surprised if some Magic Mike wannabes graced my presence, though.

After my fifteen-minute shower, I toweled off, threw on a cotton bralette and a pair of panties, and a white linen button-up shirt with a pair of short black yoga shorts and knee-high socks. I had left my towel wrapped around my long brown hair to let it dry naturally a bit; I hated blow-drying my hair—would have added to the already-excessive frizziness.

I walked out to my laptop bag in the kitchen to grab the mock-up draft of next month's magazine issue. I still heard Gen's shower running, so I slipped back into my bedroom, closed the door, and sat cross-legged on my queen-sized bed. Nothing like being surrounded by a sea of a white down comforter.

We got a mock-up of next month's issue ten days before it went to press, as all the staff writers had to ensure their stories appeared in print how it was intended to; that way, there were no surprises or discrepancies that were too late to fix. I made a few notes directly in the mock-up, labeling the issue with pastel-colored sticky notes, then a light knock sounded on my bedroom door followed by Gen peeking her head in.

"Hi, love. Pizza and wine night?" she asked jovially as I took note of the fact we had put on similar nightwear, and her hair was also wrapped in a towel.

Smiling in adoration, because she knew the way to my heart, I said, "That sounds wonderful." I salivated as my stomach started gurgling, realizing I had skipped lunch today when my nap ran a little longer than anticipated.

"Napoletano's?" she suggested, raising her eyebrows a few times and nodding, knowing all too well the pizza place wasn't up for discussion.

Napoletano's was a Neapolitan-style pizza place around the corner that was our favorite. Locally owned, it had been a staple in Dorchester for generations. We loved getting the prosciutto and arugula pizza with a caesar salad. Their sauce was to-die-for—the perfect blend of crushed, fresh tomatoes, oregano, garlic, basil, and their secret ingredient of thyme and lemon they let me in on—as long as I didn't publish it in the story.

"You know it," I said in approval. "Want to call it in?"

"Sure thing!" she said, already calling their number and closing my bedroom door behind her.

I finished up my notes in the mock-up, from headline tweaks to design issues, until I heard Gen call out that the pizza was here. I closed up the magazine, stuck it back in my laptop bag, and headed to my en suite to quickly pull the towel from my head, letting my hair fall to one side, and giving it one last towel rub before quickly brushing it.

I stepped out of my bedroom to find Gen pouring two glasses of red wine and pulling plates from the cupboard for the pizza. I walked over to the island where the pizza was, lifting the cardboard lid up, and taking a whiff of the aroma radiating off of it. Salivating, I picked up one of the plates Gen had sitting next to the box, pulling out two slices onto my plate.

"Thanks love for ordering and pouring me a glass of wine, looks delicious as always," I said smiling and picking up one of the wine glasses.

"The pizza or the wine?" she said smirking, taking a big gulp of her wine.

We always had Meiomi Pinot Noir on stock at the apartment. It's the perfect mid-tier red wine—not too dry, not too sweet and drinkable any time of the year.

I turned, looking over my right shoulder and said, "Both, of course."

&

"That's my girl," she said, following me to plop down on the floor in front of the couch. "Bon appetit."

We both started chowing down on our pizza, intermittently taking sips of wine. After a few bites in, Gen turned to look at me.

"Look I know you hate birthdays, so I appreciate you stepping out of your comfort zone to let me plan a celebration for you. You've seemed a little distracted lately, anything else bothering you?" She took a sip of her wine and continued eating her pizza as she patiently waited for my reply.

I had always been the introverted one, and although I tended to be on the more quiet, reserved side, Gen always knew when there was something off with me. We had always been connected in that way.

Holding my wine glass up to my mouth, I asked rhetorically, "I guess I'm not good at hiding things...am I?"

I took a sip as she said nonchalantly, "Not the slightest. So, c'mon, spill it."

"Well, I talked to my mom earlier this week and something seemed off with her. She just didn't seem...herself. I asked her if she was okay, and she gave me some 'never been better' generic reply, but I don't know. I can't shake it."

My mother Esmée was a big part of my life—the only part for a while. She had raised me as a single mother since I was a baby and taught me all there was to know about putting love into your food and appreciating it. She was an expert at baking but could make just about any French delicacy imaginable. She was my world, but she seemed worlds away as she had lived in Paris since I was in college. I had never been to Paris, ironically enough; she always came to visit me. Ever since college, she had made it a habit to visit Boston at least twice a year. But it had been seven months since her last visit, and even though we talked at least once a week, she hadn't mentioned plans for when she would visit again.

Although Gen usually liked to keep the tone light and fun, I knew I could also depend on her to console me when necessary. "I'm sure there is nothing to worry about. You know if there was anything wrong with your mom, you would be the first to know."

And she was right. My mother and I told each other everything and just like that, I gave a shoulder shrug and said, "Yea, I guess you're right."

We polished off the rest of the pizza and wine as she began talking about her flavor of the week—aka all the guys she was currently dating at once.

two

There are different types of grievers—some put on a brave face and can bury their feelings down so deep they didn't even know they were feeling them, and well, others, they wear their hearts on their sleeve, and you end up wearing their grief with them.

I tend to bury mine.

It seemed easier that way—that is until every emotion I had ever felt all dredged up at the most inopportune moments.

My life revolved around food and writing. As a little French-American girl, or probably any little girl I would imagine, it was always my mission to find my *raison d'etre*—my purpose for existence. I figured by the time I was twenty-five, I would be this hot-shot magazine writer in New York City for Vogue or Cosmopolitan, or something of the sorts, living in my city loft apartment, and preparing myself to be a wife *sooner rather than later.* That was somewhat a stretch from my actual life.

I often had nightmares that stemmed from childhood. My therapist described it to me as PTSD after my father died. Although I didn't remember much about him, somehow not growing up with one led me to distrust men and gave me lingering insomnia. I had tried all kinds of sleeping meds, but none of them seemed to really help. The recurring nightmares always reflected abandonment—whether it was images of my father dying, Gen leaving me, or my mother dying. And last night's nightmare was no different.

My alarm sounded, jolting me awake from last night's nightmare. Maybe it had been my conversation with Gen that spurred it, but I had a nightmare that I was sitting at my mother's funeral. It had felt so real, so frightening, that when I woke up I clutched my chest, feeling my heart racing. These nightmares caused me so much anxiety, and I typically had physical symptoms from the beginning of my day, which is another reason why I needed naps just to get through them.

The smell of coffee beans slipped into my nostrils, and I threw the covers off, hoping I could forget about that nightmare. *My mother is okay*, I kept telling myself.

Sluggishly sliding out of bed, I stretched my arms up and behind my back, before padding out of my bedroom and into the kitchen. Somehow Gen always went to bed after me and woke up before me. I wasn't a morning or a night person. I was a whenever-I-got-sleep kind of person.

"Good morning, love. Coffee or mimosa?" she asked as she poured herself a mimosa—one part OJ, two parts bubbles.

"Hmm...tough choice. Since it is Saturday, how about I start with a mimosa. But I got it. I need more than a splash of OJ, and I don't trust you," I said, sticking my tongue out playfully.

"Hey, as long as you join me, fine by me," she trailed off as she reciprocated my playfulness by mimicking my reaction. "How'd you sleep?" She asked as we both took a seat on either side of our small two-top kitchen table.

Gen knew I had chronic insomnia, and I think asking me that was her way of saying *you politely look like shit*. I told her I had another nightmare, but I had a feeling she wouldn't help ease my feelings of uneasiness that this nightmare stirred inside of me. I was too much on edge.

After taking a big gulp of her mimosa, she asked, "Do you want to talk more about what this nightmare entailed?"

Contemplating her question, I figured I'd keep it to myself because what good would it do saying it out loud. "Ahh, it was nothing. Don't worry, I'm fine," I lied, taking a sip of my mimosa.

"Okay, doll, whatever you say. Just remember, I'm here for you," she comforted me.

My lips formed a small smile as I wholeheartedly knew Gen would be there for me no matter what. Because she has been there for me over the last eight years. Through every heartbreak, through every stressful moment at the magazine, for every funny moment, she was there. But this nightmare felt too real, and some part of me felt like bringing it to life through words would make it even more real.

"We need to get out of here. We don't want to be late to your birthday dinner," she said with a wink.

The last week has flown by quickly, and although it had only been a week since she brought up planning my birthday after catching me in nap-mode, knowing her it wouldn't be anything less than spectacular.

Gen thought I was born yesterday and probably had already forgotten that I knew about the surprise birthday party she planned for me on this glorious Friday night. She had sent a mass E-vite out to the office, accidentally including my email.

"Oh, right, the birthday dinner," I said, less-than-enthused. I tapped on my iPhone for the time, which read five o'clock on the dot. She was definitely more punctual than me and probably cared more about my birthday than I did, too. I threw my hand up and twirled it in a circle to show my mediocre excitement. "Let's get the party started then."

"Whoohoo, let's go!" Gen chanted.

We rode the subway back to our apartment, and I repeated my ritual of throwing my laptop bag on one of the island counter stools, heading to my bedroom to find something to wear—which was in any case difficult. I skipped the shower since I worked at the office today and apparently crunched on time per Gen's request.

"Calling an Uber in thirty!" Gen called out from her bedroom, not giving me much time at all to clean up the mess that I was. Getting an Uber after work on a Friday night was not ideal.

I'm a food writer, not a fashionista. My idea of good clothing is Banana Republic or J.Crew—maybe I even throw Gap in there. Don't get me started on my hair and attempting to paint my face with what normal women call *makeup*—something I wasn't too familiar with or skilled at.

August in Boston is perfect weather, usually. Low-eighties during the day and mid-to-high sixties at night.

I skimmed through my closet and found a black satin midi slip dress with a horizontal neckline that still had the tag on it. *Guess I didn't go to nice places much.* I ripped the tag off, took off my work clothes and shoes, and slipped on the dress. I tapped my chin before kneeling down in my semi-formal dress and rummaging through the neglected parts of my closet—which was eighty-percent of it.

Now, what shoes was I going to wear? Pulling out a pair of classic block ankle strap heels that went with just about anything, I raised them in the air, deciding they would work best with my dress. The feeling of satisfaction over finally finding a pair of shoes to wear was short-lived when I stood and turned to find every other pair of shoes I owned scattered around me on the floor. I think being single and not dating much lends itself to not knowing what nice pieces of clothing and shoes I actually owned, since they were hardly ever used.

I did a once-over in my full-length mirror, shrugged my shoulders, and said to myself, "This will do." Now I only had twenty minutes to fix my hair and face. I always go with easy but classy hairdos and natural makeup—when I *have* to wear it. Not trying to have my face three shades different than my neck slash actual skin—or drawn-on eyebrows. My pale skin didn't match any makeup anyway. As for my face, I just touched up the makeup I had on for work: light brown eyeshadow from my Urban Decay

Naked Two Eye Palette, mascara, a stroke on each cheek of light rose Tarte Amazonian Clay blush, and a swipe of clear lip gloss. I threw my hair in a low, loose bun with slim strands of brunette hair trickling off to the sides. Rubbing my lips together, I took another quick look at my hair, especially the back with a compact mirror. After I was satisfied, I felt the look was *classic.* Exactly what I was going for.

"Time's up!" Gen shouted as she barged into my bedroom.

She looked me up and down and whistled at me with a great big smile to follow. "Well, someone cleans up nicely."

She was wearing an olive green asymmetric satin cocktail dress that had an off-center hemline and a halter neck that dropped into a cowl neckline at her chest. She topped the outfit off with a pair of nude heels and a matching clutch. Only her lightly bronzed skin tone could pull off such an outfit.

"Oh, come on. You're making me blush," I joked. "And you look absolutely stunning as always."

"Thanks, Doll," she said, winking.

Gen called the Uber, which picked us up at six-fifteen.

Gen tapped her phone screen. "Right on schedule."

"You never did tell me where we are going," I said, inquisitively.

"It's a *surprise.*"

I thought to myself, *no it's not,* well the surprise party itself wasn't, but I still had no clue where we were going other than supposedly a fancy restaurant. I also thought *I'm a journalist; we don't like surprises.* Gen should know this.

About ten minutes into the ride, I saw Gen text someone. Must be the notification of our arrival to the *surprise* party.

We pulled up to a building on Federal Street in the financial district of downtown right at six-thirty.

"Your timeliness is impeccable, you know that?" I was impressed but not surprised as I looked over at Gen.

"Yes, I do," she said with a cocky tone.

"Also, this doesn't look like a restaurant. You know I gotta eat, right?"

"Listen, we have been best friends for eight years," Gen declared. "Of course I know that. Now, let's go."

We thanked the Uber driver and got out of the car. We walked up to a building that looked like the Boston Public Library. I was very confused to say the least.

When we stepped inside, there was a bellhop standing by the elevator. "What floor, misses?" he asked, very properly.

"Nine please," Gen answered.

"Very well, miss." The bellhop called the elevator and hit the nine button when the doors opened. We stepped into the elevator and he said with a smile, "Enjoy your evening, ladies."

"Sooo..." I said, "where are we?"

"Just a little more patience. We are almost there," she said, unable to hold back a grin.

The elevator dinged, the doors opened, and we arrived on the ninth floor. When we walked out of the elevator, there was a white backlit sign on a blue accent wall that read, "Cloud Nine." *A little cliché.*

As we walked down the hallway, there were pink neon lights all the way down but even more noticeable was the dead silence. We finally reached the end of the hallway, which was pitch black for the most part.

"You ready?" Gen asked, mischievously. She has the go big or go home mentality with everything she does.

"I guess?" I said hesitantly.

She opened one of the double doors, and we walked into a pitch black room. *Here it comes...*

"SURPRISE!" I heard a group of people shout, as Gen turned the lights on.

I acted surprised, of course. "OMG! Gen, you have really outdone yourself."

"Only the best for my bestie. Were you really surprised?! " she asked, then pulled me in to kiss my forehead.

"Totally!" I lied to make her feel better about being able to pull it off. "Thank you so much, I love you." But that part was genuine.

The only people there besides Gen were coworkers. I am quite the introvert who likes to keep to herself. Gen was truly my only close friend in Boston, and I was more than thankful for our sisterly bond, especially since all my family—well, my mother—was in Paris. After the *surprise*, all my coworkers generously helped themselves to the cocktails and hors d'oeuvres after briefly pretending they were there to actually celebrate my birthday, not for the free food and cocktails.

The venue was gorgeous. Champagne and pink colors elegantly shined around the room but not as shiny as the many chandeliers that hung from the ceiling. There were candles and greenery all around, setting up the intimate vibes. Right when you walked in, there was one of those social media decorative walls that was bright pink and lined with greenery garlands. My ditsy coworkers, pretty much the entire fashion department at the magazine, lined up one-by-one for their turn at taking multiple photos. *This was definitely a Gen-planned party.* After walking around and taking in the decor, I stopped at the bar to order a drink.

"What're we having, birthday girl?" a dashing Ryan Gosling doppelganger asked with a wide smile causing a blush to further accentuate my cheeks.

"Hiii," I said awkwardly. "I'll take a Cosmo, please." I smiled back. I worked *a lot*, and it's not every day a man like that looked at me *like that*.

"Cosmo, coming right up." He handed me my drink and told me to have fun, flashing me a wink that made me want to drop my panties right then and there.

Was this going to be fun? Ehh...it's not really my scene, but I wanted to at least pretend to have fun for Gen's sake. I took my drink after lingering a little too long at the bar and made my rounds of saying hi to my coworkers I could really care less about—and I was sure the feeling was mutual. Other than Gen, I hadn't gotten to know my other coworkers well, because I was in and out of the office so much on assignments.

"Hiya, Juliette!" A creepy bald man popped up in front of me out of nowhere. That was Bob—B Magazine's circulation manager. All Bobs and circulation managers seem to be creepy.

"Hey, Bob."

"So, how's it feel to be the big three-oh?" He mouthed the 'three-oh' and held up the numbers with his fingers. *God help me. What a nerd.*

"Oh...you know...feels just like yesterday, Bob." Right at that moment, Gen saved me by walking up and looping her arm through mine, thankfully.

"Jules! There you are, birthday girl! Sorry, Bob. But, I have to show her something," she said, pulling me away, leaving Bob with a disappointed look on his face.

"Thank you," I mouthed when our backs were turned.

Lightly bouncing on the balls of her feet, Gen said, "Anytime, girl. So, how do you like your party? Do you love it?" Oh how I wish I was as enthusiastic all the time like Gen.

"Yes, of course!" I faked.

"Great, because I have more in store." She winked. "Did you check out that hot bartender?"

"Oh, boy, can't wait. And yes, as a matter of fact, I did. He made me this delicious Cosmo," I said, raising my glass.

"My girl." She nodded her head while biting her lip. "Well, you have fun, my dear. I'm going to take a photo at the wall over there, and I'll circle back with you in a little bit!"

"Sounds good!"

Gen was definitely having more fun than me. I typically enjoyed these types of parties because I rarely went to them, so they were fun while they lasted. But since that nightmare still shook me, all I could think about was how nice the cloud that was my bed would be right about now minus the hot bartender. I'm sure he flirts with all the girls, like they all do.

The sound of a metal utensil clinking on a glass caught my attention. Gen was standing on a small stage to the left of the bar holding a champagne flute.

"Can I please get everyone's attention," she said into a mic after calling everyone's attention up front. We locked eyes as I wasn't standing far from the stage. "Everyone, please grab a champagne flute. They are making their way around."

A waiter with a tray of champagne flutes made his way to me as I grabbed one from the tray and mouthed, "Thank you." Gen continued her speech once each person was holding a flute.

"I just want to thank everyone who made it out tonight to celebrate my best friend in the whole world." She raises her glass in my direction. "Jules, we have been through a lot together...mostly good." The room laughed briefly before she continued, her gaze never leaving mine. "You have been there for me whenever I needed you, and I could only hope I've done the same for you. You're the sister I never had and the lifesaver I never knew I needed. You're my cubicle buddy, the only other person I know who eats pizza and drinks as much wine as I do, and listens to all my bullshit while keeping me straight but never making me feel judged. Here's to eight years of friendship, thirty years of memories, and a lifetime more to go. I love you, Jules. HAPPY BIRTHDAY!"

The room of people clapped and cheered, joining her in wishing me a happy birthday, yet hers was the only one that mattered to me.

I let her words soak in and realized she was not only my closest—and pretty much only friend—but she was my *person*. Her words meant so much to me, and for some reason, really made me miss my mom. At that moment, I realized I hadn't heard from her, and my heart sank. My mother would have never not called to say happy birthday to me.

But I didn't have time to dwell on this fact before Gen hopped off stage and walked toward me, embracing me in a tight hug.

"Thank you so much, Gen...for that speech...for all of this," I said, waving my glass around the room and gulping down the last remnants of the champagne. "Really, I love you."

"Ahhh, you know I love you, and you so deserve it! Let's get a photo at the booth soon, yea?" she asked when I started feeling my phone buzz in my clutch purse.

"Sure, let's do it," I said as she took my hand and started pulling me toward the photo wall.

My phone started buzzing again, and I tried to ignore it, but it rang a third time. I pulled it out of my clutch, and the caller ID read *Margot Moreau*. Margot was my mom's best friend. So my heart started racing, my palms were sweaty as it had to be an emergency for her to call me, especially at twelve-thirty on a Saturday morning. I got a bad feeling in the pit of my stomach and told Gen I'd meet her there. I spotted a pink sofa at the back of the room and called her back immediately.

"Hello, Margot, is everything okay?" She was hysterical, and all I could hear were sobs on the other end of the line before she answered.

"My dear, Juliette, no...no, it's ta mère..." she paused for a few seconds, letting her tears do most of the talking.

"What...Margot...what's happened?" I pleaded.

"She...she's gone chérie..." she said, matter-of-factly while still distraught, trying to find words through her choking sobs.

My heart started beating fast, and I dropped the phone. I held onto the arm of the sofa I was sitting on and placed my hands over my mouth, not completely digesting the news that was just broken to me.

Picking my phone up off the floor, I managed to say through a strangled voice, "What do you mean she's gone, Margot..."

My heartbeat was galloping inside my chest. I couldn't get a full breath of air as I listened to the cries on the other end of the line that should be mine.

"I'm so sorry, darling. She begged me not to tell you. But, she's been...sick."

"What do you mean sick? What kind of sickness, Margot?"

"Cancer. She was diagnosed with terminal ovarian cancer a few months ago." I briefly thought back to the realization that my mother hadn't made plans to visit. Because she had known she wouldn't be alive long enough to.

"What...no...she would have told me. I don't understand." I couldn't wrap my head around what Margot was telling me. My mom had cancer and no one told me? Other than Gen, my mom was my best friend. The only family I had left. There is absolutely no way she had been diagnosed with terminal cancer and didn't tell me—and there was absolutely no way she was just *gone*.

"It's what she wanted, Juliette, I'm sorry," she apologized again, as if it would wash away the pain, betrayal, and shock I was feeling.

I realized at that moment my nightmare wasn't a nightmare—it was a warning signal, a premonition of my worst fear.

I had a one way ticket to the place where all the demons go. *Hell.*

three

*"Jules, Jules...*what happened, are you alright?" I could hear Gen asking me in the background, my ears were ringing, and the room was spinning.

I could hear Margot yelling the same thing out of my phone that had fallen out of my sweaty palm onto the ground.

"Gen...it's my mother...sh–she's gone," I stuttered, having trouble finding the words, the strength to utter *my mother is gone.*

Margot hung up, and I could see my phone lighting up, over and over again, as she attempted to call me back after dropping the phone. I couldn't talk to her anymore—at least not right now. I couldn't even begin to describe how angry it made me. I didn't even have a chance to say goodbye...to my mother...who just died from cancer. A cancer diagnosis I no idea about.

"What do you mean...she's gone?" Gen repeated the words I had just said, also not understanding what they meant.

"I mean my mother died from cancer, which I had no fucking idea she even had. That's what I mean." The words were flowing from my mouth so quickly I couldn't breathe, and I damn sure didn't understand what I was saying...what was happening. The shock coursed through my body in a way that made it not be able to produce tears. I also didn't want to cause a huge scene at the party, completely falling apart on the outside as I was on the inside.

I knew she seemed off when we talked last, but I would have never imagined this.

"Holy shit. Jules...I don't know what to say." Because what could she say?

My mother wasn't hit by a car. She didn't commit suicide. She didn't have a sudden heart attack, yet her death felt *sudden*. She had a slow-dying disease—although incurable, this wasn't sudden. She had the opportunity to tell me she was dying, to make sure I had said my proper goodbyes to the only family I had left. But she didn't. And for the life of me, I don't think I could ever wrap my head around the *why*.

"Say you'll go with me to Paris to help me figure out this mess..." I couldn't wrap my head around what was happening let alone jump on the next flight to Paris to process it all by myself, but I knew that's what I was going to have to do—but what I needed Gen to do with me. I was always a planner, and it usually helped ease my anxiety. So, even though my mother had just died, this was no different.

The magazine would have to do without us for a little while.

"Yes...of course I will. No questions asked." Gen wrapped her arm around me as I sat on the pink velvet sofa at my thirtieth birthday party too stunned to cry about the *sudden* death of my mother.

All the feelings rushed over me: anger, hurt, disappointment, sadness, confusion. How much didn't I know about my mother, and how much was I about to unfold? I may not know now why she didn't tell me she was dying, but I needed to find out. First things first: I needed to book a flight to Paris.

My mother and I had a close but complicated relationship. When I started college, she moved back to Paris and our communication became naturally less frequent. My mom raised me as a single parent and never told me much about who my father was—other than he died.

We lived in Chestnut Hill, and when I was in kindergarten, I realized all my friends had their dads take them to school, for the most part, on their way into Boston for work. One day, I came home from school and asked my mom, "How come I don't have a daddy, Mommy?"

Her reply was, "Oh, moi gentille fille, he died when you were just a bébé." I never asked many questions about who he was, and on the rare occasion I did, my mother's reply would be, "Ce n'est pas important chérie," in other words, 'that's not important darling.'

Although my mother was born and raised in Paris, her English was decent when she moved to the United States in 1991 and unfortunately didn't use her power of bilingualism to teach me French fluently. She spoke to me in her mother tongue some, but never in full sentences and never with the purpose to teach. I understood some words here and there but not enough to fluently speak it. The one thing she did teach me: how to cook and appreciate food—very Parisenne of her.

The saying she lived by was: "Surround yourself with people who love food as much as you do, and you'll be in good company." Food was her love language she had passed on to me. I grew up watching my mother glow in the kitchen when she mastered a recipe passed down from many family generations, moving around elegantly and with purpose. Food brings people together. The French know this, and they cherish the time they get to spend with each other over a meal—especially a delicious one. And the moments I got to spend with my mother cooking and/or baking I will cherish forever.

You see, food isn't just food to the French. We never understood the whole "food for fuel" thing as eating is an orgasmic experience for us. We savor every bite we put into our mouths, and that is something I very much inherited from my mother—from our French roots and culture.

In France, food is seen as a pleasure; there is no guilt attached to enjoying our food. No foods are off-limits, and yet everything is consumed in moderation and in smaller portions, sitting down and without rushing through our meals, savoring every bite until there is nothing left on our plates. It is considered *rude* to not finish what one puts on your plate, according to the French.

From Kindergarten age, I would sit at the kitchen counter just watching her, studying her, as she masterfully prepared all the French classics for every meal. For breakfast, she was waking up at the crack of dawn to prepare dough for fresh baked Pain Au Chocolat, croissants, beignets, every sweet and savory crêpe you could imagine, or Croque Madame—and any other French-baked goods under the sun. For lunch, it was Soupe à l'oignon (French Onion Soup) with a fresh and colorful salad. For dinner, it was a charcuterie spread to start, then Coq au Vin or Confit de Canard, maybe Ratatouille, and a chocolate soufflé for dessert. These were just a few of the French delicacies my mother whipped up for me during her time in America. I was spoiled with some of the finest foods from inception, until I went to college that is.

My mother met my father while he was on a business trip in Paris. Once she graduated from culinary arts school, she moved to Boston to be with him and opened up a French bakery in Chestnut Hill, a Boston suburb, called *Frangipane*. When my father died, she continued running the bakery, as it was a huge success and staple in the Chestnut Hill community—and where I spent most of my upbringing. That's as far as the story goes—or, as far as she would tell me—when it came to my father. I didn't even know his name. I guess what you don't know can't hurt you.

As I got older, my mother told me she had my bassinet and baby walker close by the kitchen at all times in the hopes I would pick up not only her love for cooking but her skill. I sure did pick up her love for food, but as for the skill, you just can't compare to someone's native cooking and their personal love they put into each dish—not for the lack of trying, though. I could not get the smell of fresh baked bread and chocolate out of my nose, even if I wanted to. I remember walks with her in the Public Garden on the weekends and nights when she would braid my hair before bed; there was always something so comforting about that gesture—about our bond. Like I never even needed a father, because she provided everything I ever thought I could need as my mother.

She was my best friend, and the only person in the world who knew everything there was to know about me besides Gen. She was the only family I had left, and now, she was suddenly gone. All of the memories I had of her flashed by in seconds, which is now all I had of my mother—just memories and lost hope.

Before our flight to Paris, I went to my favorite secret spot in Boston that overlooked the Seaport. It was a secluded grassy area at the top of a hill that had a small, squared concrete slab with a short wooden plank in the middle. I'd sit there and reflect with my journal, writing down whatever I had felt in the moment. But this time was different. I couldn't pinpoint how I felt now, as all the emotions I had felt just a few hours ago turned to numbness.

My mother's death launched my second identity crisis. The first was finding out who I was without a father, and now I was really lost, trying to find out who I was without a mother. She shaped all the best parts of me, and now she was gone—something I could have never prepared for. But then again, how could I ever know who I am without knowing where I came from? I realized more than ever my father's abandonment through his death affected me to my core, so much that I blamed my mother for abandoning me, even though she didn't have a choice. But she did have a choice to tell me, and that still made it feel like abandonment.

I was left with the lingering questions: Who was he? Who am I? Why did she do this? Why did they do this? They all started and ended with him. I was left with nothing but more uncertainty about my life than I ever had before. All I could think was why did everyone I love leave me.

four

The nearly eight-hour direct flight from Boston to Paris had me recollecting and relishing the distant memories I had with my mother, especially five Gin and Tonics-deep. Gen kept me company, and I was thankful to have a best friend like her in a moment like this—a friend who would drop anyone and anything to be there for you, no matter how big or small the task was. In reality, I had nothing else. I had no family left, I had no boyfriend—now I had to take time off from work, one of the few things left in my life that I loved that I could control and found absolute joy in.

Writing gave me the outlet I needed to deal with the things I could never change. Ever since I was in middle school, I kept a journal. I would just scribble about my park walks with my mother, how I never felt like I fit in anywhere, how I didn't have a dad like everyone else. Putting pen to a piece of paper made me feel seen and heard, and that just felt good. Like I was creating something just for me, and that in itself was beautiful. Sprinkle in a love for food I inherited from my mother, and my journalism career was basically decided before I even knew I could make a living out of eating and writing.

"Maybe you should slow down a little bit, Jules," Gen said, trying to mother me after I slugged back my fifth Gin and Tonic, like it was water. It sure tasted like water.

I knew I shouldn't have tried to medicate with the Devil's Juice, but I was trying to keep numb, because I was afraid of how I would feel once everything soaked in. I still hadn't wrapped my head around not ever seeing my mother again. Her beautiful brown hair and golden brown eyes, and a smile that never made you feel like she was hiding anything from you—but apparently I had read that wrong. But she was all I could see when I closed my eyes, and the thought of her—of never seeing her again—caused tears to well up in my eyes as I forced them shut.

"It's all good. I don't need a mother right now, Gen. Well, fuck. That's ironic how that came out. But you know what I mean." I shook my head and regretted the dizzy feeling it gave me immediately. "I need a friend. And as my friend, show a little understanding that I'm going through a rough patch with my mother just dying, and I need a little alcohol therapy," I bit out, pinching my thumb and index fingers together, running an air zipper across my mouth, hoping she would get the hint with my unnecessary—and childish—hand gestures.

"Understood." She sat back in her seat and put her headphones in her ears after muttering her short, one-worded comment.

I shouldn't have been so rude to her; I knew she was just looking out for me, but I was hurting. I didn't hurt much when it came to not having a father, because I really didn't know him nor did I know what it was like to even have one to begin with. He died when I was so young that I couldn't really remember what the few moments we shared together were like. But not having my mother around, that was uncharted territory for me that would take some time to navigate, to understand, to heal from. Although from the looks of it, I didn't really know her at all, either.

I mimicked Gen and also put my headphones in, sitting in silence most of the flight, alcohol in hand and staring out of the tiny airplane window that made everything down below look so small. And it was symbolic of the way I felt: *small*. I knew any words to escape my mouth wouldn't have come out the right way, and Gen shouldn't have to be the victim of that carnage, so I settled on keeping my mouth shut the rest of the plane ride, drowning in my temporary alcohol fix.

I chose to hurt in silence, from the death of my mother, from her lying about being sick, from not being able to save her, for being on the way to say goodbye to her ashes—not her body full of life I already missed so much. With no grandparents, or parents left to call family, I was forced to try to lean on the living who aren't my blood. Did that really mean anything anyway? Gen was the only person I could count on to not leave me, and I mean, she wasn't my blood. Nothing made sense, and everything I had believed in before was suddenly unbelievable.

I must have drifted off since I was abruptly awakened by the overly bumpy plane landing. I looked over at Gen who appeared to be sleeping also, before she was awakened by the landing, too.

"Looks like we made it," she said, eyes fluttering open and lighting up by the sight of the glimmering Eiffel Tower. Even in the daylight it's a masterpiece.

For a half-moment, my eyes lit up, too, until reality shook me from my reverie, and I remembered why we were here.

When Gen and I made our way off the plane to baggage claim, I felt like I was on auto-pilot. I remained numb—I'm sure it was a mixture of shutting down emotionally from the death of my mother and all the alcohol I had just consumed on the flight—well, at least it did what I wanted it to, *temporarily*.

After we collected our bags at baggage claim, there was a black town car waiting out front with a driver dressed in all black next to it holding a sign that said, "Mademoiselles Juliette et Genevieve."

We approached the driver who was an epitome of a French town car driver. He had a black cab hat on, clear glasses, mustache, and a little patch of facial hair under his bottom lip...can't forget the bushy sideburns.

"Bonjour, mademoiselles, mon nom est Bernard," he said in a thick French accent, as he opened the passenger door for us and took our bags, barely being able to stuff them in the backseat and trunk. Two women traveling to Paris for an undetermined amount of time did not equal light packing. "Mademoiselle Margot, make sure I take excellent care of you two. We are headed to Miss Dubois's chalet. Make yourselves comfortable." Miss Dubois is...was my mother.

"Wonderful. Thank you, Bernard, and lovely to meet you." He smiled back at me, nodding in response, a look of pity owning his features.

I hadn't been to my mother's new chalet, as I had never visited Paris, and absolutely hated that I would be seeing it for the first time under these terms—without her even there. Work was always crazy, and the only traveling I had been doing, if any, was for work. My mother understood this, so she visited twice a year when her schedule allowed.

Bernard drove us to the chalet, which was located in the heart of Paris. It was almost sunset, and Paris was preparing for fall foliage and cozy weather. Gen and I didn't say much to each other on the way to the chalet, as we were both taking in all the beautiful sights, although the sight of my mother in my mind was everywhere I looked, overshadowing what my eyes were actually looking at.

My mother met Margot when she moved back to Paris after I started at BU; she sold the *Frangipane* Boston location and opened up a location in Paris. Margot owns and operates a pâtisserie nestled in the historic center of Paris near the Eiffel Tower, *Pain d'Amour,* which translates to "Bread from love."

Frangipane was more of a la pâtisserie (pastry shop), while Margot's Pain d'Amour was classified as a boulangerie, in which she sold more baguettes, sandwiches, and crêpes rather than pastries, desserts, and other baked goods like croissants. That's why Margot offered to let my mother sell her mille-feuille in her shop.

They had been best friends for the last twelve years—ever since my mom had her first bite of Margot's mille-feuille: a to-die-for French layered puff pastry and cream dessert. They became business partners not long after, and Margot let my mom in on her secret ingredients: dark chocolat and frangipane. Mom didn't have the heart to tell her that her palate was so refined she could *taste* the not-so-secret ingredients but let Margot feel they shared that secret anyway—after all, my mother did own her own French bakery back in Boston...named *Frangipane*

Margot's mille-feuille was her specialty dessert that she would make fresh every morning for my mother to sell in her display case. It featured layered puff pastry and cream, and depending on where you got it, was the artsy part of it; some had raspberries or strawberries in between the layers, others decadent chocolat swirls on the top. Margot's had both.

Bernard helped Gen and I grab our suitcases from the town car and walk them up the short cobblestone pathway leading to the cottage. Beautiful shrubs and colorful seasonal flowers guarded the front yard of a two-story cream-colored cottage with a chestnut brown door and powder blue shutters, with a thatched roof and chimney. It looked like there was an attic floor due to the single window on a third level. The cottage appeared to have been built in the early 1900s and has since been renovated and preserved by my mother. It was a charming cottage in a cul-de-sac of other much larger homes.

We thanked Bernard for helping us with our bags, and I opened the front door to the cottage, followed by Gen gasping.

"Oh my God, Jules, this is the cutest little cottage!" I think by her excitement she had forgotten that we weren't technically here for a vacation but a memorial service.

Although the chalet was adorable, it was hard for me to get excited about it. My mother had kept the original gas stove and chimney, which gave way to the log fireplace. The shabby-chic vibe was different from how my childhood home was decorated. Maybe she wanted to go with a shabby-chic vibe so she could keep some of the chalet's charm but add her own cozy yet modern aesthetically-pleasing allure.

The chalet reminded me of the Rosehill Cottage from *The Holiday*—it was a movie my mother and I watched every year together during the holidays when she would come to visit. In addition to the original little white gas stove, the kitchen cabinetry was shaker-style and the same powder blue as the front door, matching the floating shelves that displayed an assortment of vintage china, and a distressed off-white kitchen table made for two. The living room was also cozy and decorated with cream and blue accents, and the cottage's original gorgeous cobblestone fireplace. Up five steps of a small staircase, there was also a reading area with shelves of books and a reading chair, decorated with a throw blanket and pillow, two bedrooms and two bathrooms. The master bedroom had the en suite and fireplace.

"Yea, it is." Gen rolled her eyes at my monotonous response and put her bags in the secondary bedroom.

I was surprised she let me have the master, but at least she remembered why we were here. All I wanted to do was run a hot bath in the luxurious standalone tub and wash away the fact I was going to my mother's memorial service. I could feel her presence as soon as I walked into her home, taking note of her reading glasses on the side table next to the reading chair, the faint smell of Chanel N°5, the way she had her throw blanket folded over the sofa, the dishes left out drying on a mat next to the kitchen sink—it all just felt like she would be coming back to her home soon. But that was an illusion I would have to transfer to reality.

five

The back of her wavy brown hair caught my eye.

"Mom!" I called out to her, but she was too far away. "Mom...Mom!" I called out again, this time louder.

She turned to face me, and her fair skin glowed in the rays of sunlight. She is so beautiful and just as I remembered her. It had only been seven months since she visited me in Boston, and according to Margot, she didn't know she was sick then.

Her rose-colored lips and pearly whites smiled warmly at me with her golden brown eyes that always seemed to smile, too, because they were so full of light. She was wearing her cream-colored coat with a herringbone collar and a sheer, light brown neck scarf—neck scarves were a staple accessory for her.

"Jules...is that you, darling? What are you doing here?"

"I came for you, Mom." She just smiled again and cocked her head to one side.

I placed a hand on her cheek, and it was stone cold.

"Jules...I'm scared." Her frightened face started to disintegrate into a pile of ashes, every last cell of her being falling to the ground.

I closed my eyes shut as the tears fell into my open hand that had just cradled her face a few moments ago. Before I knew it, she was gone.

The nightmares were worse now that she was gone. But I didn't expect any less. Her death was yet another traumatic experience for me, and I wasn't sure how to process it all. On top of that I had to try to sleep in her bedroom; her ghost might as well have been standing in the room with me.

It was my mother's wish to be cremated; we weren't religious, but we were spiritual.

"Spread my ashes along the Seine River, Juliette," she told me randomly not long before she passed away. "Like my love for you, it will always flow."

I didn't understand why she even brought it up, but I do now. That must have been one of the first hints that pointed to the feelings I had of something not right with her. I didn't know how I didn't see the signs in the way she talked, the distance she slowly started putting between us the last seven months of her life. She called less and appeared more busy; I'm assuming because she had a lot of oncology and chemo appointments. And the fact that she willingly hid them from me hurt more than anything. Maybe my anger was starting to consume the grief.

The funeral home was different from what you would expect one to look like. There were rows of dark brown, wooden individual seating—I'm sure thousands of others had sat in as they had said their final goodbyes to their loved ones—wood plank floors matching the color of the seats, and a smell of death you couldn't place. The walls were painted a light teal color, with intricate crosses embellished in each column panel on either side of the triple-pane windows that lined the space. It reminded me more of an event space than a funeral home save for the crosses.

There was a large canvas photo of my mother sitting on a white easel that was decorated with an array of white flowers. Her urn was situated on a wooden pedestal beside the easel. It was beautiful and embodied who she was—golden, simple yet elegant, opal and iridescent. All the shades of white around me signified purity and sympathy.

Bernard, our wheels and unofficial tour guide, had taken Gen and I by a flower shop on the way to the funeral to pick up a small bouquet of red anemone flowers, which symbolize death or forsaken love. I thought both meanings were fitting. I had placed them next to her urn when Gen and I spotted Margot.

She embraced me in a hug, and without any words from either one of them, we took our seats as the service was about to commence. They were on either side of me and both took one of my hands with a light squeeze of reassurance. The gesture made me feel a little less alone.

The funeral celebrant started the service. Soon afterward, I had been expected to say a few words, which hadn't even crossed my mind. All of a sudden feelings of unpreparedness washed over me—unprepared for my mother's death and unprepared to speak at her funeral. It was overwhelming.

"Without further adieu," the celebrant commenced, "Esmée's daughter would like to say a few words." *Would I?*

She waved for me to come up to the podium that was to the left of her photo and urn.

I looked to my right at Margot, who had pursed lips and gave me a *you can do this* nod. Taking a deep breath and shutting my eyes briefly, I steeled myself, having no idea what I was going to say. I stood from my seat and made my way to the podium. When I reached it, I placed my hand at each side of it and stared at about thirty people I had never met before.

I focused my gaze on Gen and Margot, who had grounded me at this surreal and uncomfortable moment, before I began, "As some of you may know, my mother raised me by herself. I never knew my father, but she always made me feel like I didn't need one."

Scanning the crowd, it was a sea of black clothing, solemn looks fixed on me. The sad faces turned to pity with each word I spoke. My gaze paused on one man's face because of the way he looked at me when I said *I never knew my father* was odd. Although I didn't recognize him, I was curious who he was. He was a man in his fifties, sitting in the same row as Margot and Gen but on the opposite side of the aisle. His eyes were crinkled and filled with hurt, almost like a look of pity like the others in the room but not quite. I had never met him before, but for some reason, I was drawn to the way he looked at me. I looked back to Gen and Margot before I continued, both of them nodding in that way that showed me I could continue whatever it is I was about to say about my late mother.

"I never respected or loved anyone more than I respected and loved her. She was my best friend, the woman who dedicated her life to making sure I had a good one, even though it wasn't always easy. She had a heart of gold and would go out of her way to help anyone in need. She taught me how to be graceful in everything I did and to love unconditionally. She will be forever missed by me, by her best friend Margot, and anyone who had the pleasure of knowing her. I love you, Mom." I managed to make it through the whole speech—that came straight from the heart—but looked over to Margot, who couldn't contain her tears. I still felt the shock of what was happening and wished I could cry like that, but I couldn't.

She was holding a crumpled up tissue as I made my way from the podium back to my seat next to hers.

I decided to omit the part that I didn't even know she had cancer, because I wanted her image to be preserved with dignity. Although she didn't tell me, it registered with me that she deserved that. For all she had given me, for all she had done for me, for the way she loved me, not just as one parent but as two. I was grateful Margot volunteered to organize the service since I had to travel in, and I honestly don't think I would have been able to process having to plan all this.

At the funeral reception, which was in the room next to where the service was, Gen and I were talking about how beautiful the service was but how we didn't know anyone else there besides Margot. I caught the man, who gave me that unsettling look during my speech at the mention of not having a father, staring at me briefly a few times, then would turn his head when our eyes met. He was charming and had shaggy light brown hair with specks of gray to match his facial hair and crystal blue eyes. How did he know my mother? When I made my way toward him, my steps were interrupted by a familiar face. Margot.

"Mademoiselle..." she couldn't hold back her tears as she pulled me in for a tight hug.

"Ahh, Margot." I hugged her back, letting the hug linger as I held her tightly.

I didn't know Margot that well as I never came to visit Paris, but she reminded me so much of my mother. I could understand why they became best friends: their smiles and natural warmth about them could ignite a strong calming effect in the hardest of times. They both also had impeccable taste from food to fashion to interior design. And much like my mother was, she is stunning and classy. She has collarbone-length dark brown hair with subtle caramel lowlights, dark brown eyes, and a slim figure that was usually dressed in Chanel or Dior. Her straight, white smile could light up any room along with her an airy, charming French accent were unmatched.

"That was a lovely speech. Your mother would have been proud. How was your flight, darling?" I ignored her question, still fixated on the man I didn't recognize. Gen just stood next to me, wordless.

"Margot, who is that man over there?" I asked, not able to take my eyes off of him.

"Monsieur Leo? Didn't your mom tell you, chérie?"

"Tell me what, Margot? Who is he?" I pleaded for her answer.

"Oh, Jules that is...was...your mother's...Leo..."

I placed a hand and clutched it over my stomach, as I suddenly felt sick at how little I knew about my mother. Exactly how much had she been hiding from me?

"Umm, no, she didn't," I uttered, smiling tightly, although I was less-than-amused—a French faux pas. "Who is...will you both excuse me?" It wasn't a question but a demand, rather, as I made my way toward Leo.

"Jules...wait. Where are you—" Gen said as she lightly grabbed my hand.

"I'll be right back," I said, pulling my hand from hers.

I walked up to the man, who looked like he was bracing himself for a disaster.

"Umm...excuse me...I think you knew my mother..." I skipped formally introducing myself first, as my anger over the situation washed away any manners I was taught. "I noticed you've been looking at me and I just...well, I..."

"Juliette." He said my name in a way like he knew me without having to introduce myself. "I have heard so much about you, and Esmée boasted photos of you, but I must say, you are much more beautiful in person. You remind me of her." He had that look again—something of a mixture of sorrow and understanding for the loss I was experiencing, but there was something else there also that I couldn't place. I hadn't expected him to be American, either.

"That's interesting, because I have never seen photos of you. In fact, I've never even *heard* of you, Leo, is it?" I couldn't help but add a little bit of sting to my words. I didn't hear about him, and all I could wonder was *why*. And how...when did she meet this American man?

"I understand how this may make you feel, Juliette, meeting me on these terms, and I begged Esmée to tell you, but she insisted it was best to keep *us* on the quiet side." His words stung more than the words I uttered, because how could he possibly understand how I was feeling?

"I...uh...I need to go," I stuttered, my voice shaking.

"Juliette, wait—" He tried to gently grab my arm, to hold me there, in a place I couldn't breathe, in a room that was spinning as I tried to drown out the noise of chatter from people I didn't know talking about my mother, who I also didn't know, apparently.

I rushed out of the funeral home, not caring about Gen or Margot, or whoever the fuck that Leo guy was. When I slammed my hands through the double doors that led to my exit, to escape from a horrible nightmare, I was outside, but I was still gasping for air.

I thought I was having a panic attack, as I tried to breathe through muffled sobs. My chest felt tight, nausea rose up to my throat, and beads of sweat formed on my forehead. I paused, clutching my chest, then ran farther down the cobbled road until I felt safe enough to stop. Finally, I was feeling something.

six

Esmée

As I was writing a letter to my sweet Juliette, I reflected on where the time had gone. I wasn't honest with her that I was dying, among other things. I didn't want her to remember me that way.

When I found out about my diagnosis a few months ago, there wasn't much time left. *Terminal ovarian cancer.* I was in the final stage. I knew something was wrong when I didn't want to cook—to eat. Knowing my love for food, how could that be? *C'est la vie—that's life,* I suppose. That was just the beginning of the brutal symptoms I was destined to experience. One night I had the most excruciating pain followed by a bout of blood on the sheets.

I'm so sorry, but you have cancer, the doctor told me. *I will refer you to an oncologist for further evaluation. I know this wasn't the news you were hoping for.*

We are looking at two months, maybe three, was what the oncologist told me.

I felt numb, like the world was moving on without me while I stood stuck in time, stuck in his words.

Juliette was all I've ever lived for. I decided not to tell her about my cancer diagnosis—or about Leo. I figured it would open the door to her asking about her father again, and I couldn't face her when she was supposed to finally find out about him.

I remember naming her Juliette. It means youthful, beautiful, and vivacious in my French culture. When I held her in my arms for the first time, the most innocent and precious baby, I just knew she would be all those things, and she surpassed my vision of who she would grow up to be. I was beyond proud of the woman she had become, and I knew I was leaving this earth cognizant that my job was done.

The letter I was to include in my estate for Juliette hurt me more than the cancer did. I would take physical pain time and time again if it meant I could spare Juliette the hurt of reading this letter instead of me telling her the contents. But instead, she would learn of them from a stranger, my estate attorney.

Knowing my daughter, she won't take it well, and that thought killed me quicker than the cancer was going to. I hope one day she will forgive me and understand why I did what I did. I always held myself to a high standard, with grace on the outside and the secrets I had been keeping on the inside. Nearly thirty years I had been holding these secrets that are undignified, unforgivable in my mind and in my heart.

The only thing worse than being afraid of dying is being afraid of how the world moves on without you after you die. I have so much unfinished business that this thought scared me more than anything.

My *dear Juliette*, I'll love you more than you'll ever know, and everything I ever did was to keep you safe, secure, to keep you guarded from the evils of the world. If I ended up creating an evil in the process that I couldn't protect you from, I would never forgive myself. I hope when you find out—because you will—that you remember how much I loved you unconditionally, and I can only hope you could love me without condition, too.

seven

Three months. That's how long I was legally allowed to stay in Paris without a visa. We were to fly out this evening, but I felt there was too much unfinished business. So, I considered taking a leave of absence from the magazine.

The last thing I was supposed to do before we left was have an appointment with my mother's attorney to go over her estate. I figured this would be a cut-and-dry event, but little did I know, it would be far from it.

I knew she came from money, but I never knew to what extent, since she wasn't close with her family; I never even met my grandparents. My mother told me that after she left Paris to be with an American man—my father—her family wasn't keen on the idea and chose to cut her off while she lived in Boston. However, when my mother moved back to Paris when I started college at BU, she reconnected with her parents. Only for them to die in a horrible car accident two years later, before I had a chance to meet them. Since my mother was an only child, they left her their inheritance and the family chalet—the cottage Gen and I had been staying in.

"As per your mother's wishes," her attorney, Raphaël Allaire started, "you are the sole proprietor of the chalet, which was appraised at $1.9 million Euros. Your mother also had an additional $10 million USD in capital. She left *Frangipane* to Margot Moreau, which was already discussed with her. She also left you this..." he said matter-of-factly, sliding an envelope across the mahogany desk in his office.

Although the room had been overwhelmingly warm, it suddenly felt ice cold. Time was moving forward, decisions were being made, and I was trying to move with them while feeling numb again.

And just like that, I owned a home in downtown Paris and inherited millions of dollars—I had no idea how to handle either. My mother left me everything as expected, and a letter. I figured she would leave her pâtisserie to Margot and wholeheartedly respected that decision, because although we spent many days baking together when I was a child, I still didn't know the first thing about running a business, let alone all the pastries they could make.

"Thank you, Mr. Allaire," I said, stuffing the white envelope in my bag. No matter what it said, I wasn't going to read it in front of a stranger.

He nodded in understanding with a tightly pressed mouth.

I rushed out of his office and back to the chalet, so I could read it in private. I had no idea what was written in the letter, but it may have been the last thing my mother ever wrote, and that alone sent shivers up my spine. I had a feeling the letter felt as cold as what was written inside it.

My heart was pounding, and I was glad Gen was out sightseeing. She was worried about me after I left the memorial service abruptly. When I finally found my way back to the chalet later that night, Gen was already in her pajamas.

"WHAT THE HELL, Jules? Where have you been?!" She had scolded me, a look of concern glazing over her usually soft features.

"I had to get out of there...I was...I had a panic attack," I explained.

She stilled, mouth falling open. "Oh my God, are you okay?"

I explained to her how meeting Leo threw me over the edge. She understood and pity filled her eyes.

Pulling myself out of recollection of that night, I poured myself a glass of Bordeaux and headed up to my room. As the lukewarm water filled the giant standalone tub, I tried to collect my current thoughts. I wondered how many times my mother sat in this very tub, if she sat in here, contemplating whether to tell me about the cancer, about Leo, about my father, about whatever else she had been hiding.

When the water filled close to the brim of the tub, I gently set my glass of wine on the floor and dropped the letter next to it as I undressed. I dipped my toes in first then lowered the rest of my body in, soaking up all the warmth I could.

I reached over the tub and picked up my glass of wine and the letter, twiddling the thin piece of paper in between my fingers in between sips of wine. I decided I wasn't ready to open it quite yet.

After getting out of the bath, I got dressed, and sat on the edge of the bed, holding the letter in between my shaking hands once again. I had to tell myself it was now or never.

Slowly tearing open the envelope, I unfolded the letter that was inside. It smelled like her Chanel perfume but also reeked of disappointment.

The letter started off with my mother saying how much she loves me and everything she ever did was for my benefit, how she wishes she was brave enough to have told me in person the words on the page that changed everything for me.

She said she told me that my birth father died when I was three years old, but the truth was, she lied about it. She didn't want me to grow up thinking he didn't want me, according to this letter she wrote on her deathbed. She thought it would be easier to know he left my world without the choice to stay.

He isn't dead.

He's alive.

He's out there somewhere, waiting for me to find him or not caring at all if I do.

What hurt the most is that I heard the story about my father from a letter—not my mother. My mother told me she met my father while he was on a business trip in Paris for a month. At the time, she was in culinary arts school at Le Cordon Bleu Paris. Once she graduated, she visited my father in Boston and never left. He helped her open up *Frangipane*. My mother told me he died when I was two but never shared the details—now I know why; it wasn't true.

Who was this woman? I was starting to feel like I was living in a twisted reality that wasn't mine. How was I supposed to grieve my mother and be furious with her at the same time?

My emotions were spinning into oblivion. My chest felt tighter, as I brought my hand to it to ground myself. I let the letter slip out of my hand and fall to the floor along with my belief she had good intentions for putting me through this special kind of hell. I put both of my frigid hands on either side of my face, tears and shame filling them.

I was betrayed by the person I loved most, and she wasn't even around for me to tell her how much it hurt me. I found the courage to pick the letter up off the floor to finish reading it.

"Be the light they thought had burned out. I'm sorry I didn't tell you about my illness. I thought it would be better this way. I knew there wasn't much time for me left, and I didn't want you to remember me this way, chérie. I hope one day you will forgive me and see why it had to be this way, Juliette. I love you more than you'll ever know, and I know you'll know what to do with what is left."

I was left with no choice but to decipher what all this meant. It was too much. She said she trusted me with this information, and that I would know what to do with it, but I don't—at least right now I didn't. Do I go searching for answers—for my father? She didn't give me much context of who he was...who he is. Do I go about my business and do nothing? I found myself processing the grief of my mother while trying to undo the grief of my father—a man I had been craving my whole life to see, to know, for the last twenty-seven years, and for some reason she thought it was best to keep this from me. *Twenty-seven years.*

I have faint memories of my father. His wavy brown hair, crystal blue eyes that admired his baby girl, the stubble on his face that lightly covered his cheeks like sandpaper when he held me, the way he smelled of musk and sandalwood. Then...all of a sudden...he wasn't there anymore. I was left with only a faint memory of him.

The number of people I had left in my life and whom I could trust were dropping like flies. All I knew was that my father might still be alive. The rest was up to me if I even wanted to find out who he was...is. Was it too late?

The letter made me go back and forth in my mind and in my heart: should I go back to Boston, or should I stay because I needed more time to figure all this out, to collect my thoughts and feelings.

I stood from the bed, taking note of the sliver of moonlight that crept its way through the bedroom window. I walked over to the window while inhaling a deep breath, exhaling out the negative air within me. The sight of twinkling city lights from the Paris skyline contrasted with the night sky above it. The Eiffel Tower was prominent from my bedroom window with orange lights that lit it up from top to bottom. Looking for a sign of my mother in the stars, the illuminated moon reminded me she would always be with me, because I was sure that wherever she was, we shared the same one. I found a slight comfort in that.

Nothing made sense right now, but I had a feeling in due time it would. Or, at least I hoped it would.

I had fallen asleep on top of the duvet in the chunky knit sweater and jeans I had on the previous night—the letter my mother had left me clutched to my chest with a throw blanket covering my face. Moving the blanket down and the letter to the side, my eyes flitted open thanks to the small ray of sunlight beaming through the window as the sun rose up.

I laid there for a minute wondering what I was going to do next; this letter my mother left me had me questioning my next move.

A knock sounded on the bedroom door, breaking up my fleeting yet haunting thoughts. "Hey, Jules?" Gen said, hesitation lacing her tone.

I took a moment before answering, deciding if I wanted to pretend to still be asleep, but I decided to speak, "Yea?" I said with a low voice, staying where I was, leaving the door as a barrier between my personal space and the outside world for just a moment longer.

"Can I come in?" she asked, her voice quivering.

"Yea, sure." My eyes fixated on the door, as I laid on my left side in a fetal position, my hand still placed over the letter.

Gen turned the knob, cautiously entering the forbidding room.

"How are you holding up?" She asked with furrowed eyebrows and a slight frown, a look of concern taking over her features as she sat on the bed beside me, softly running her hand across my calf.

"I'm okay...how was sightseeing?" I responded unconvincingly, though Gen accepted my answer and change-of-subject question, not pressing, beknowing exactly how I was *holding up*.

I know people have a hard time reassuring loved ones through a time of grief and never know what to really say, because what can you say?

"It was wonderful. I went to the Louvre, the Eiffel Tower, the Musée d'Orsay, Cathédrale Notre-Dame. Absolutely stunning architecture and work of arts. Wish you would have joined me."

"Yea...me, too. Sorry I had to meet with my mom's estate attorney."

"Gotcha. I know that must have been a lot. But I understand you wanted to do it alone. What do you have there?" Her eyebrows raised, eyes on the letter that remained under my hand, as she tipped her chin toward it.

"It's...my mother...she left me a letter," I struggled to say, as its contents plagued me the night before.

"So...did you read it?" I knew her journalist curiosity couldn't refuse to press any longer, as I would have wanted to know what it said, too.

I explained to her that my mother confessed that she lied about my father dying when I was young but really didn't go into the details of *why* she lied about it. That she willingly hid her cancer diagnosis from me for months, that one day she hoped I would forgive her.

"Jules, I'm sorry. On top of everything else, I know that must be a heavy weight you're carrying. Let me know what I can do for you," she said, and I could feel the sorrow she felt for me, as she didn't have many words to say—which was out of character for

Gen—water pooling at the edges of her eyes, her upper body folding over my lower body, the side of her face resting on the side of my thigh.

"Thank you, Gen. Means the world to me. Your friendship...means the world to me," I said, all the while void of emotion. "I think I need to...stay."

She sat up quickly, staring at me for a moment, wordless. We had been in Paris only a few days now, only planning to stay for the memorial service and for my meeting with the estate attorney when I had first heard of the news.

But, after reading this letter, I really couldn't leave—not now.

"Oh?" was all she managed to vocalize.

"I just need some more time, Gen. My mother left me this chalet, and I need to make sure all is taken care of here and what to even do with it," I explained. It was only a half-lie.

I needed to retrace my mother's final steps before she died and spend more time with Margot—and Leo—to see if there was anything else I was missing, feeling like I was having to get to know my mother's latest version of herself through others who apparently knew her better than I did. It wasn't enough for me. And as a reporter, I knew I had to go straight to the sources.

"I'm going to take a leave of absence from the magazine," I said with a strangled voice.

Late last night, sometime between reading the letter and falling asleep, I had sent our editor an email explaining I would be taking more time off work until November. She understood and sent me the paperwork required to request a leave of absence. I filled it out sometime between receiving the response and finally falling asleep.

"Do you need me to stay an extra few days with you?" She asked, knowing she would if I wanted her to. But I wasn't so sure I did.

"I think I need to figure this one out on my own, Gen. I appreciate you so much, though. Thank you for the offer."

I did appreciate her. She had always been a great friend to me, but I needed my own space to sort through what my mother left me with—and all the emotions it left with me.

"Of course, Jules. I'll always be here for you. I love you, doll." I nodded in understanding, before she hugged my lifeless frame as we embraced the next few moments of silence, and she packed for her departure.

And all of a sudden, I was going to be alone—and not just physically.

eight

ffter taking an hour-long nap following Gen's departure, I decided I needed to get outside for some fresh air. Before I did that, though, I needed to make a phone call. I dialed Margot's number and apologized for rushing out of my mother's memorial service. I felt like the abruptness was somehow a symbol of how my mother left me. It was a part of me now.

"Hey, Margot, you got a minute?" I said after she picked up.

"Jules...of course I do, dear. How are you?" I was getting tired of people asking me that when they knew the answer, but I knew it was just a polite gesture I was going to have to get used to for a while.

"I'm holding up. Thanks for asking. I wanted to let you know I decided to stay in the city a little while longer. I thought it would be good to spend some more time here while I can and just allow myself time to grieve in the last place my mother was. Three months to be exact. That's how long I have before my temporary visa runs out, anyway."

"I see and definitely understand why you would want to. Let me know if you need anything at all, Jules. I'm here for you, darling, anything you need." I thought some damn answers would be nice, but I wanted to ease into that conversation. There is a time and place for everything.

"Thank you, Margot. I greatly appreciate it. Well, I'm about to head out for a walk, so I'll catch you later." I didn't want that phone call to last any longer than it had to.

"Yes, cherie. I recommend taking a stroll on the Pont des Arts," she suggested.

"Thanks for the recommendation, I'll check it out. Bye, Margot," I said before she said her goodbye.

"Au revoir, Jules." I desperately hung up the phone.

It was hard for me to face my mother's best friend, because she reminded me so much of her.

I changed out of my sweatpants into a pair of high-waisted jeans, a plain white tee, and a pair of white Cole Haan sneakers. I called Bernard to see if he could take me to where Margot suggested I take a walk.

The Pont des Arts in Paris is most famous for being the love lock bridge, where tourists and passersby attach personalized padlocks to its railing and throw the keys away in the Seine River.

Grabbing my small Chanel hobo crossbody—one of my many high-end gifts compliments of my mother—and the chalet keys, I headed out the door where Bernard was waiting out front for me.

"Where to, mademoiselle?" he asked me after I opened the passenger-side door and slipped into the seat of his black town car.

"The Pont des Arts, s'il vous plaît," I requested before he pulled out of the carport.

"Yes, madame. Good choice," he said, smiling and driving off to my awaiting destination.

Bernard dropped me off at the wrought-iron Pont des Arts bridge entrance, opposite the Institut de France. It was simply magnificent. Margot was right; it truly is a lovely part of the Seine River with the Louvre Museum on one side and the Institut de France on the other.

Upon research, I had learned the Institut was originally built as a college for students from conquered states, the building included a public library and a chapel. The building presented baroque decor and strong symmetrical design at its center, the chapel, with a grand entrance and dome. It was how I would picture a palace, a European architectural masterpiece. It boasted many windows, and although I didn't make it inside, I imagined what the natural light was like. A French flag waved in the breeze, above the building's clock in front of the dome, and I observed a massive gorgeous light stone building with mansard roofs, at the end of the bridge from a distance, as I slowly made my way across.

Tourists and residents flooded the bridge as I took in the thousands of locks that lined it, a sea of color, as I walked toward the Institut. I wondered about the souls who had passed by, leaving a lock behind and what the simple action meant to them. Were they couples visiting that were leaving their mark in a foreign place, or maybe a mix of locks from residents who had a place to return to remember past and current love?

I paused at an unfiltered spot on the bridge, staring out into the endless blue river, arms hanging over the bridge's ledge. I reveled in an introspective moment with myself—thinking about what I truly wanted out of my time in Paris. What answers were I searching for? Was I crazy for staying? Did I really want to know what else my mother may have been hiding, or should I leave well enough alone? Before my thoughts deeply threatened my mental state further, I was interrupted by a male French accent from behind me.

"Visiteur américain?" he asked me.

I turned around to face the man interrupting my peaceful reverie. "Excuse me?"

Being interrupted had annoyed me, at first. All I wanted when I came here was a moment of peace to myself. I wasn't in the mood to be nice to a random Frenchman who assumed it was okay to call me out on my apparent look of being an *American*. I didn't know much of the French language, but I knew enough from overhearing my mother's conversations with others to carry a general conversation. Also, if he knew I was American, why was he speaking to me in French? I thought to myself. These thoughts and feelings were fleeting, however, when I really took him in.

Pierre was a charming man in his thirties, shaggy but tamed light brown hair to match a light stubble that accentuated his chiseled jawline, and light eyes that speckled into a fossil gray with hints of hazel when the dimming sun hit them in all the right places. And the accent...

"Ehh, so I was right. So, you're not from around these parts. Mes excuses if I was being rude. The name is Pierre," he said, holding out a hand toward me.

As I left his hand hanging in the still air, I stood dumbfounded for a moment before offering my name. "Jules."

I held out my hand to shake his hand after a few beats of contemplation on what his angle for interrupting my thoughts was, but at the same time, I was flabbergasted by how attractive this perfect stranger was.

When his hand wrapped in mine, I felt a jolt of electricity pulsate through me as we locked eyes for a brief moment before letting go.

"So...Pierre—" I was cut off by his need to correct me.

"It's Pi-ehr...not Pi-air...but close enough." He smirked, showing off his straight, beaming white teeth, thinking he was cute or something—well, I mean, he wouldn't be wrong.

There was something playful about him, but at the same time, I couldn't decide if I was vibing with it or not. Maybe it was my conflicting feelings of grief and excitement.

"Excuse me, Pi-ehr," I started emphasizing the roll of the "r" at the end of his name. "As I was saying, is there something I can help you with?"

"Not really." he shrugged. "Just admiring a beautiful américain woman when I see one." I must have had a bewildered look on my face, because his warm features turned to amusement.

"I see...well if you will excuse me, I was a little *busy*, you know, appreciating my space and alone time here," I said, a little surprised in myself that I was denying this beautiful Frenchman, but I wasn't here for that; I was here for solace.

And for answers, and this man would only be a distraction, possibly the best kind but one I didn't need right now nonetheless.

"Understood. I'll carry on then. I'm sorry to have bothered you," he said, nodding and walking past me toward the Institut.

I was surprised he took the hint so quickly. I stared at his back for a moment as he walked away, still not understanding what just happened, as he turned back to look at me for a moment, flashing a quick smile again before continuing to put distance between us.

I turned back to look at the river, perfectly content with where I was at that moment, the sound of tourists' voices all around but feeling a peace and quiet in being alone, too. A flash of orange and purple illuminated the sky as the sun was almost completely down now.

After I was satisfied with what I came here for—just a little ounce of solitude in my great war—I called Bernard to pick me up, but I wasn't ready to go back to the chalet, yet. Where I would have to face the ghost of my mother.

When Bernard asked me, "Where to, mademoiselle," I felt the hunger grumbling in my stomach. I realized I hadn't eaten all day.

"Frangipane, s'il vous plaît, Bernard," I told him, knowing just the place I could get a quick bite to eat.

"Oui, madam. You got it."

nine

On the drive to my mother's pâtisserie—the one she left to Margot in her will—I had learned Bernard was *my driver* for the duration of the trip. He dropped me off in front of Frangipane and told me to let him know when I was ready to head back to the chalet. I thanked him and stepped out of the town car onto the sidewalk.

I think Frangipane closed around four in the afternoon, but Bernard had told me Margot stayed later to clean up and make sure the shop was ready for business the next morning.

Frangipane took up residence on the tree-lined Avenue des Champs-Élysées. It had a mint green storefront with an embossed black banner with gold lettering that read *Frangipane* adorning the signage. The most adorable street lamps were hanging off black hooks on the side of the building, greenery and white flowers dressed up the second floors' windows with shutters the same color as the rest of the storefront, and a delicious, tantalizing window display of French desserts and pastries. On the front door of the bakery, there was a wooden sign with a jute loop hanger, marked "Closed," so I hesitated to reach for the door handle.

But that's when I saw a familiar face in the display window.

Margot had just picked up a pie to remove from the window area before looking up at me. She set the pie back down and waved for me to come in.

I took a deep breath in before twisting the gold knob on the front door she had just unlocked. As I walked inside, the traditional door bell sounded.

Margot was still smiling as she softly shut the door behind me and locked it again. It appeared she was alone here. "Jules, what a lovely surprise."

"Hey Margot, I hope I'm not bothering you. I just came from the Pont des Arts and was hungry so thought I'd just stop by here. Thank you for the suggestion by the way. It was just what I needed."

"Not a bother at all," she said, still smiling genuinely. She looked tired, but she was still beautiful and warm. "I was just cleaning up, but I'd love to whip you up something.

"Are you sure? I wouldn't want to impose," I said, half-meaning it as my stomach was not happy with me.

"Absolutely, dear, come with me." She smiled again before gesturing to me to follow her into the kitchen.

When we slipped past the white door with a small, circular window that led to the kitchen, it was immaculate. White railroad tile lined the kitchen walls, stainless steel appliances and marble countertops full of bakeware pieces situated strategically, whisks and spatulas of every kind hanging on one of the walls—not an item was out of place. It had my mother's touch written all over it. There was also a small four-top kitchen table at the corner of the kitchen farthest from the door, and I imagined my mother sitting at it, working on her books and accounting after a long day.

"So, this is la cuisine...where the magic happens." Margot lit up as she said that, clearly radiating the fact that this was her passion, just like it was my mother's. "Please, have a seat," she said, waving her hand toward the four-top table and throwing her apron on.

I took a seat at the chair facing the kitchen, so I could watch her cook. She moved around just as my mother used to, flawlessly and elegantly, passionately and with ease, devotion and excitement with every small movement. For a brief moment, I had a flashback of when I was a young girl sitting at the kitchen table doing my homework, watching my mother move just like Margot had, humming to music in the background. It was a sweet sound and a blissful sight. The memory made me smile.

Margot quickly brought me back to the present moment. "How does a feuillete au jambon sound?" She asked, already turning on the oven and pulling out ingredients from the large stainless steel fridge.

"Sounds wonderful, thank you."

As Margot started kneading the dough for the savory puff pastry she was making me, there was a brief silence before I asked, "So, Margot, I was thinking...I could use something to do while I'm here."

"Oh?" was all she responded with, patiently waiting for me to explain.

"Well...can you maybe...I don't know, teach me how to bake? Maybe I can help you out here since I'm sure you're bogged down with Pain d'Amour already?" I asked, hoping she would take me up on my offer. I figured this may be the first step to truly understanding who my mother was, by exploring the one thing apart from the people in her life that she cared for the most.

"Ahhh, I see. Well, of course, dear, if you would like to. I would love to teach you my recipes. And I could always use the help. Your mother would be proud of that, you know? She always loved my mille-feuille, you know." She smiled voluminously, not taking her eyes off the pastry braid she was preparing to stick in the oven, brushing egg wash on the top of it, but I could also sense a pang of sadness in her voice at the mention of my mother.

"Awesome...and I appreciate that, Margot," I said, feeling like I was home in her embrace as she welcomed me into her space, well, my mother's space, with open arms.

This was my mother's pastry kitchen that she built from the ground up, and I suddenly felt a wave of missing my mother, forcing the sting of tears at the back of my eyes to stay put. Margot put the feuillete au jambon in the oven, and we sat in silence as she cleaned up.

The timer sounded after thirty minutes, and Margot pulled the decadent ham and cheese pastry from the oven, setting the baking sheet on the counter. She pulled a spatula from the wall, slipping it under the twisted braid, as my stomach grumbled and my mouth salivated. She slipped it on a plain white plate, walking it over to where I sat, gently setting it on the table in front of me.

"Bon appetit," she said, smile never wavering as she sat down next to me.

"Thank you, Margot," I said, taking a bite of one of the most delicious things I had ever tasted.

Essentially, all it was was ham and Gruyère cheese wrapped in puff pastry—but again, she had a magic touch, just like my mother—and there is nothing like sweet or savory breads in France. With one bite, it melted in my mouth, so soft, buttery, and cheesy. Just the comfort food I needed after failing to feed myself.

"Bonne?" she asked, as I nodded and scarfed it down, piece by piece, pleased with herself. "So, dear, how are you holding up?" She asked me for the second time that day.

That clearly was a rhetorical question used to pass the time, so all I replied with was, "Okay."

We talked for about an hour—not about my mother's death—but all the places I should go while I was there and the plan for me to work with her. For a moment, she brought my mother back to life through her smile. I could envision them sitting across from one another just like we were doing and just talking about life.

After I pointed out it was getting late, she walked me to the front door. "I'm glad you stopped by, Jules. See you at seven a.m. for your first baking lesson?"

"Yes, me, too. See you then," I said with a tight-lipped smile.

She smiled back before closing the door behind me and locking up. I waited for Bernard, who was just around the corner, feeling like I could make my time here mean something, rather than sulking around searching for answers I may never get. He scooped me up, and we headed back to the chalet.

I thought to myself on the drive home that maybe instead of searching for the ghost of my mother, I could embrace her world—trying to see it as she saw it. Maybe then I would get the answers I was looking for.

My mother was running as I called out to her, "Mom, wait, stop!"

She turned back to look at me, a frightened look etched on her face, running faster and faster away, closing the distance between us. What was she running from?

I couldn't catch up, and I stopped running after her. She had disappeared from my sight.

My alarm sounded, thankfully breaking me away from the nightmare. I tapped on my phone screen: it was 5:30 a.m. I wasn't so sure I wouldn't be able to get up this early every morning, but this time I did so with grace, knowing I needed to do something to fill my time other than mulling over the letter.

I limply rolled out of bed and stumbled to the ensuite bathroom. I stared at the long brown hair falling dully over my shoulders, sad hazel eyes with just a tint of light still reflected in them, sunken dark circles lining them, and my pale skin that could use some more sunshine. I took a moment to realize I was staring at a version of myself grieving the loss of her mother.

I shook away the tears threatening the back of my eyes and picked up my hair brush, brushing through the knotted clumps that had formed in my sleep. I pulled it back in a high ponytail, brushed my teeth robotically, and applied a little concealer and mascara to the face I no longer recognized. I threw on a pair of jeans and a white tee, as my wardrobe consisted of predominantly neutrals, and slipped on my white sneakers.

As September neared, the mornings were cooler, so I grabbed a light gray cardigan before calling Bernard to pick me up. He said he was already outside waiting for me. Damn he was good.

As we headed to Frangipane, a chill ran up my spine as I recalled the nightmare I had last night. Who, or what, was my mother running from? Maybe the truth.

"Here we are, mademoiselle. Enjoy...the baking with Madame Margot. I'll be back here at four," Bernard said, as he pulled up to the side of the bakery, a smile beaming across his face, causing his mustache to straighten momentarily.

"Merci, Bernard. Au revoir." I smiled back as he tipped his black cab hat and chin toward me.

I stepped out of the town car, checking my watch as I approached the front door. I was a little early, but I'm sure Margot would appreciate that. Being a journalist, we understood the importance of keeping our word and our deadlines. As I walked inside, a flood of delicious and warm aromas entered my nose, my stomach growling as a result. Margot had already started baking. I took in the sight of the well-lit bakery cases that lined the counter, displaying beautiful sweet and savory pastries; it screamed pastry food art—croissants, cakes, you name it.

"Bonjour, chéri," Margot said, smiling as she walked out of the kitchen, pushing a stainless steel cart through the swinging door that contained multiple levels of baking sheets with just croissants on them.

"Bonjour, Margot," I said, forcing a smile.

One, because my mother just died, and I still wasn't sure how to find happiness living with that fact. And two, because I wasn't a fan of being up so early.

"You ready to create art you can eat?" she asked excitedly in her French accent I thought was so sweet and genuine. How could someone be so bubbly this early in the morning, I thought.

Baking was a religion to Margot and my mother—a religion that was practiced every single day, wearing an apron and flour. Her passion for baking was brilliant and infectious, and it made me long for a time where I could be standing here beside her. The times we used to spend in the kitchen when I was younger, the love for food—specifically hers—grew the more I watched her coast effortlessly around the kitchen with happiness. I felt a pang of regret for not making more of an effort to see my mom more, to actually come visit. Maybe then I would have known she was sick. Life is too short, and that concept was just a saying to me before now. Now, it was evident more than ever.

Now, that was all I had of my mother—distant memories, and it pained me to think about them. Although I enjoyed being around Margot because of how much she reminded me of her, the realization that she wasn't her maimed my heart. I would never see my mother again, hug her again, taste her cooking again, and that feeling was foreign to me—the feeling of never.

"How could I not be?" I faintly smiled, as I received one in return from Margot that mirrored a mix of pity and eagerness.

"Allons-y alors," she said in a sing-songy voice. "In other words, let's get to it. First things first, when you come into the shop in the morning you of course turn on all the lights, and then grab an apron. Start the coffee and warm water for tea, and I like to start early on the easier of the fresh baked goods, like croissants, beignets, pain au chocolat, palmiers, then move on to my special mille-feuille, crème brûlée, and macarons and such."

Margot walked me through the steps of how to make croissants, and she might as well have been speaking French to me. From kneading the dough to adding the butter, the eggs, the yeast. How was I going to remember all of these steps?

"Then, the final step before you put them in the oven is brush with egg wash. This allows for a shiny, flaky, and attractive croissant exterior. Comprendre?" she asked as I stood there just blinking my eyes, confused as ever. No, I did not understand this process...at all.

I watched my mom bake a lot as a child and was like her little assistant, but I had never baked anything from scratch on my own. She would let me help with the final touches like adding sprinkles to the top of something, or icing, but I never had to craft something by myself—she did the cooking and the baking, and I did the eating. That's why I chose the job I have, so I could just do the eating. This whole idea of making these baked goods from scratch made me nervous, and I hadn't the slightest clue what I was thinking suggesting I could do this, or that I wanted to do this, rather.

When I didn't answer after a few beats, she said, "Uhh...maybe I just come in the mornings to prepare everything, and you help me at the register and pack up to-go orders?"

"Now that I can do, Margot," I responded, as we both smiled in agreement, and a small weight was lifted off my shoulders as she laughed lightly.

What I would give to hear my mother laugh like that again.

ten

As my stomach continued to whine from hunger—even though I didn't feel like wanting to eat—the ding of the bell that sounded when someone walked through the door startled me. I cocked my head to the side, knitting my eyebrows, trying to remember where I had seen the man who walked in before. As soon as he flashed that perfect smile, brushing a hand over his shaggy but tame brown hair, gray eyes smiling at me, too, I remembered the man I had met last night near the Pont des Arts. How could I not remember his name to be Pierre after he made a scene about me mispronouncing it.

He walked toward the display case counter, and his gray eyes continued to smile along with his lips. He stopped me in my tracks, lips parted, heart racing, as I realized he looked even more beautiful with the natural morning light flooding into the pastry shop's windows. His stubble was a little thicker, and he was wearing a pair of tapered brown pants paired with a gray long sleeve quarter button shirt that accented his eyes and held the muscles in his arms hostage.

I stood there dumbfounded as he reached the counter, still smiling, holding me captive. He radiated sunshine and seeing him again, when I never thought I would, made me feel stupid for being so rude when I met him yesterday.

"Well, well...I remember you," he said, as he lightly tapped the counter with his hands, showing off his perfect dimples as he grinned from ear-to-ear.

I realized my baker's hat was still on my head as well as my apron from my baking attempt with Margot that morning, which I took off both rapidly and embarrassingly. Tossing them on the counter beside me, I smoothed down any loose hairs that were sticking out from my ponytail.

"You..." was all I was able to let out, like he had sucked all the words out of me with one sweep of his natural charm. "I mean, yes, hi. I remember you, too. Last night at the Ponts des Arts. Pierre, right?"

You would think being a journalist and talking to people all the time would have set me up to be a smooth talker but no, that wasn't the case—at all. I was awkward as hell.

"The one and the same...*Jules*," he said amusingly, making it evident he didn't forget my name.

"Hey, Juliette, I need to run to Pain d'Amour—" Margot said, as she rushed through the kitchen door.

She didn't finish what she was saying as she was happy to see the man standing before me. Kissing him on each cheek, she continued while I stood confused. Was Margot a cougar?

"Ah, I see you've met *mon fils*," she pointed out, as she stood beside him, linking her arm with his and temporarily resting her head on his shoulder.

"Your...son?" I asked quizzically, not sure if I translated *mon fils* correctly in my scattered brain.

"Mhmm," she sounded, as I tried to digest the fact I didn't know Margot had a son. A very *attractive* one at that.

How did I not know this? I didn't see him at the funeral with her either, then again, I didn't stay the whole time. I had so many questions, so many doubts about everything I had ever known but quickly realized this wasn't the time or place to address any of them.

"We actually met yesterday afternoon, maman...at Pont des Arts," Pierre chimed in as I'm sure I had a flabbergasted look on my face, not being able to find words for this discovery.

"Ahh...one of the many reasons I recommend. My son loves to *think* there. Anyway, as I was saying, I have to run to the boulangerie, some fires to put out. You okay here?" she asked, seemingly confident in my abilities to run a pastry shop I had spent a total of a few hours in...in a foreign country. I only hoped most French people spoke English somewhat, too.

"Yes, I think I can manage." I smiled warmly as she set a gold key on the counter.

She explained deftly what to do with any leftover pastries, to count down the register, turn the lights off, and lock up if she wasn't back by four p.m.

"Got it," I mouthed, as she kissed Pierre on the cheek again, before rushing out the front door.

The bell dinged, and I was faced with this handsome man, who I just found out was my late mother's best friend's son. *What the fu—*

"So, Jules is short for Juliette?" Pierre asked rhetorically, a smile plastered on his face.

I wondered if the man was ever sad—or, maybe the incessant smiling was a front. I found myself wanting to know more about him in general.

I smirked, unsure of why he was lingering in the shop; I had assumed he only came by to see Margot. Now that she had left, why was he still here? Not that I minded he stuck around; I was just curious. That's one of the main reasons I became a journalist after all.

"Is there something I can get you?" I asked, half-being a smart ass.

"As a matter of fact, may I get a black coffee and a croissant with butter, s'il vous plaît?" He graciously responded.

"Coming right up. I baked some croissants this morning myself...for the first time, so I apologize if they aren't as delicious as usual. Actually, they will be, because I only helped Margot...your mom...make them." What the hell was I saying? My foot could exit my mouth now.

I shook my head as I took note of the still-amused look on his face and poured his coffee into a to-go cup, picked up a pair of tongs, and gently pulled the croissant from the display case, placing it in a small, pink baker's box with a few small commodity butters.

"Here you go, sir. Order's up and on the house," I said, flashing a coy smile and receiving one in return.

"Merci, belle." *Did he just call me beautiful...?*

All I could manage was a nervous smile and a nod.

"Very well, I'll see you around then, Jules." Pierre took his coffee and to-go box off the counter, and turned toward the door.

As I was not in the mood to stop him from walking out the door with everything else I had going on, a part of me wished I would see him again—soon.

I found myself picking at my fingernails as the anxiety coursed through me, though. I hadn't pursued anyone in a while, and of all times in my life, now wasn't the right time to.

A few steps away from the front door, Pierre turned around. "Jules," he started, and I was not prepared for what he was to say next. He beamed a flawless smile before saying, "So...I...uh...I figured, if you would like someone to show you around, from a local's perspective, I would love to offer up my tour guide services."

I stood there dumbfounded for a moment. I wasn't expecting that, nor was I sure I wanted his *services*.

After a brief contemplation of thinking *what did I have to lose, I probably needed to get out of the chalet more often*, I answered him, "Okay, great."

"Great." He smirked, and I wondered how often he had his way with the ladies.

However, I thought he was cute, and being Margot's son, I figured he was harmless. We exchanged numbers, and I told him I would be in touch after I got a little more settled. I guess getting that international phone plan before I left was a good call.

He turned to walk out the door, and I thought to myself that maybe—just maybe—I could get used to the kind of effect he had on me.

There was something about Pierre that had this calming effect on me, like he grounded me without even trying. He was animated and even-keeled—all the things I wished I could be but wasn't. It made me think back on the meaning of my name: *youthful, beautiful, and vivacious.* It's like my mother hoped her daughter would always be these adjectives that I didn't end up being—maybe everyone else saw me this way, but I couldn't see myself as anything other than a sad, lost woman.

I think my happiness was just so overshadowed by the loss I had experienced—starting with my father—that I couldn't fully live. I always felt like a piece of me was missing, because it was. Half of who I was died...literally. But I'll be damned if I continue to let these thoughts bleed into me trying to find a happiness I had never been more desperate to find. I wanted answers, but I also wanted to simply be happy again.

Margot ended up having to stay at Pain d'Amour, so I locked up at four on the dot. I realized I didn't pick her brain about Leo, but I also thought I was still trying to process it all, so I would have to save it for another time.

After my first shift at Frangipane, I thought I would automatically feel different, *be different.* Maybe somewhat closer to my mother, closer to clarity, to answers. But, as with anything, things don't just happen overnight. It had only been a week since my mother passed away, and I was all but ready to slap a bandaid on the hole she had left in my heart.

Bernard drove me back to the chalet, and I headed up the stairs, throwing my bag on the floor, and flopping down on the bed. All my energy had been exhausted from the last week. I had even lost track of what day of the week it was. After lying on my back for a few minutes, staring at the bubbled ceiling, I realized I hadn't heard from Gen since she flew back to Boston. It was almost five, which meant it wasn't even lunchtime in Boston, yet, so I decided to dial her number.

She answered after a ring-and-a-half. "Jules! How are you holding up, love?"

"Hey Gen, I'm hanging in there. I hear you made it back to the B okay then?"

"Oh yea, back at it. Nothing new here. You know, just your typical headlines...top five travel destinations this fall, how to pack for your 10-day European dream vacation. How exciting, right?"

"Ha! Well, it depends who you ask, I guess." I paused, chewing on my lip as I considered sharing my news. "So, I kind of did a thing..."

"Ooo...Jules, you aren't getting into fun trouble without me already, are you?" I laughed from my belly, something that felt so natural whenever we spoke, because she was such a hoot. She always found a way to make me laugh and cheer me up in the darkest of times.

I explained to her how I started helping out Margot at Frangipane, and how I met Pierre at Ponts des Arts, and then again at the shop—and how he's her son.

"That's a LOT to unpack, Jules. I'm glad you're doing something, though, while you're there...you know, to kind of get your mind off things. I'm missing you like hell, though. Oh, and tell me more about this French hottie."

"Well, he's about six-foot-one, shaggy light brown hair and stubble, stormy gray eyes, perfect smile and dimples, muscular, charming as hell, and probably someone who would never be into someone like me," I said flatly, my low self-esteem rearing its ugly head. "His name is Pierre."

"Oh, c'mon, Jules. You're absolutely beautiful inside and out. Any guy would be lucky to have you and stupid to let you go. But, hot DAMN. This man seems too good to be true...and French accent I presume?"

"You're too sweet. You know I don't deserve you, right? But, yes, total Frenchman who has me swooning...a lil bit." I blushed thinking about Pierre and when I would see him again.

These feelings I had, the grief over my mother, lightened a little bit. I was hopeful even.

I swear Gen was falling in love with the thought of him over the phone.

"Well, listen, doll. I have to get back to work but keep me updated on Mr. Perfect and take care of yourself, okay? I miss you, and love you, and don't do anything I wouldn't do. Leaves a little but leaves a lot. HA, kisses," she said, dropping off the line.

Everyone needs a friend like Gen.

As I set the phone beside me on the bed, I thought of all the reasons I should just pack up and go home. How I should accept my mother's death and stop playing whatever pretend game I was here in Paris. The past had been dealt, and my mother had made her choices. But as a journalist, I was much more focused on the bigger picture than the grueling process of getting there. Only time would tell what that process was going to look like.

september

eleven

Over the last two weeks—three weeks since my mother's memorial service—Margot had managed to teach me all the Frangipane recipes, and I was picking up speed there while getting comfortable with making pastries. Who knew a journalist-turned-pastry chef would be what became of me?

With $10 million from my mother burning a hole in my pocket, I figured I really didn't even need to work, but I needed something to do. I had all of a sudden millions of dollars in assets I had no idea what to do with. So, I had agreed to help run Frangipane for free while Margot got her ducks in a row with the acquisition of it, i.e. finances, staff, etc.

Helping Margot with Frangipane also meant that I could avoid all the loose ends I still needed to deal with from my mother's death. Her ashes had been held at Margot's house. I figured I owned the chalet, so I should just keep it and rent it out as I didn't picture using it much after I returned to Boston. There was also the whole emotional torture of unpacking all the lies my mother told me, but that end would likely remain loose for some time.

When people back in Boston ask what I did and saw in Paris, I'll tell them I learned to bake pastries—that about summed it up. I knew now was the time to say proper goodbyes to my mother, and I needed to request her urn from Margot, which she had gracefully secured until I was ready. Well, as ready as I would ever be.

I rolled out the dough in long, repetitive strokes as Margot flitted around me.

Inhaling deeply, I said, "So...Margot...I'm ready..." I trailed off

"Ready for what, dear?" she asked innocently, furrowing her eyebrows.

"It's time I said goodbye to...my mom," I finally admitted out loud to someone else other than myself.

This made it all seem real, for the first time since she passed. I was finally accepting she was gone but still had no idea what that future looked like altogether—a future without her. That vision I had as a little girl was shattered. I didn't have a father to walk me down the aisle, or a mother to help me get ready in my wedding gown. She wasn't going to be there when I had a little girl of my own—to watch her grow up and become a grandmother. These big moments I still had left in my life didn't have her in it, and that realization was devastating.

Yesterday, I listened to the last voicemail my mother ever left me, hoping to find solace in hearing her voice, but it only made me more sad that those were the last words I would ever hear her speak: *Jules, my darling. Sorry I missed you, talk soon.* Little did she know—or might have known—we wouldn't be talking soon. The same thing over and over, and it just wasn't the same. It felt robotic, because that's really all it was. I didn't want the part of me that was her to die, but at the same time, I didn't really have a choice.

"Oh..." was all she mouthed until she said, "what did you have in mind?"

"I want to spread her ashes at the Seine River. It was her favorite place in the whole world. Just me and you?" I asked her, realizing I also never addressed the Leo situation.

"I think that's a wonderful idea, chérie. But...I don't really know how to bring this up—" Margot struggled to find the words, and it was as if she read my mind, knowing she was about to bring him up. I put up my hand to stop her.

"I know what you're about to say, Margot. It's Leo, isn't it?" She nodded, and let me continue, "I just don't know him, and it wouldn't feel right...to me at least."

"But your *mother* knew him...and he was by her side the entire time she was sick," Margot cut straight to the point, and she was right.

Although I knew nothing about this man, there was one thing that was certain—my mother was in love with him, and he was in love with her, or so I thought. How could I deny him the privilege of being there when we spread her ashes? It didn't take much convincing for me to change my mind, after taking a few beats of contemplation. I am human after all.

"I have no idea how to get a hold of him..." was all I said.

"I can surely help with that." Margot smiled, satisfaction spreading across her features.

I was going to have to face the man my mother had been hiding from me—and the question still remained: *why?* However, I had to bury the curiosity, along with my mother, so that I could get her goodbye over with. Something I desperately needed to do, yet wanted to avoid at all costs.

That Friday, Margot and Leo met me at the Pont des Arts bridge that overlooked the Seine River—the same place I had met Pierre just a few weeks prior. I guess this spot was becoming a monument of significance. I also realized I needed to get settled in here and say my goodbyes to my mother before getting involved with Pierre in any way. This realization made me torn.

How could I afford to be happy when I was so sad?

Leo was a handsome man in his early-to-mid-fifties with wavy brown hair that had hints of salt and pepper to match his facial hair and blue eyes with kindness reflected in them. For some reason, there was also a hint of familiarity in them. Must have just been from the memorial service, as I've never seen him before then.

I had pictured my mother being with him—a short video played like a reel in my mind, of them laughing together, walking hand-in-hand in the park like we used to, staring into one another's eyes, sharing kisses. I wished I would have been able to witness how their love grew—and how it was at the end of her life, at least for her. But, she didn't give me that privilege. And there was a pang of immense sadness that settled within me—how I never saw her in love and never would.

Leo and Margot walked side-by-side as they approached me on the bridge. She was holding my mother's beautiful champagne-colored and gold-embossed urn that mirrored her beauty. The feelings of sorrow, grief, anger, and resentment washed over me, making me feel like I was drowning—it was all sinking in; she was gone. My chest felt tight as I took a few deep breaths, trying to prepare myself for the inevitable.

Margot greeted me, planting kisses on either side of my cheeks, before Leo opened his mouth to speak, his eyebrows furrowed. "Jules, thank you so much for allowing me to be here. I know it's what your mother would have wanted, and of course I wouldn't want to miss it for the world. I just want you to know I cared about her very much. I still do...and I miss her dearly," he said, pain behind his words that caused further pain in my heart.

Tears started to fall from his eyes and it seemed genuine as he pulled me in for a hug. His words made me freeze, and this wasn't the time to pry about why she didn't tell me about him if they did love each other this much.

I was still curious about how they met, but for now, I swallowed my need for answers to get through this moment. Right now, I just needed to be present in this moment for *her*.

I looked over at Margot, who discreetly wiped a tear from her cheek.

After Leo pulled out of the hug, I said, "Yes, of course. I'm so sorry about how I reacted at the memorial service, but I hope you understand how it made me feel learning of you...that way. I don't want to get into it now, but it did hurt. I hope to get to know you a little better, before I have to go back to Boston." And I meant that, but more so I could get the answers I had been longing for.

He nodded in understanding before he said, "No need to apologize. I completely understand. And likewise." He gave a faint smile, before Margot chimed in.

"Now that we got that out of the way, shall we say goodbye to my dear friend, Esmée." It wasn't a question, and Leo and I nodded, as we all moved closer to the railing lining the river.

I took a deep breath in as Margot removed the urn's lid, and all three of us took some ashes in our hands. It was a strange feeling, holding my mother in the palm of my hand when her presence felt so much bigger. Now, she was nothing more than sand. Sand that was about to slip through my fingers into nothingness. The thought made me nauseous, and I had to swallow it down with the rising bile in my throat.

We all nodded to each other in unison, signifying it was time to finally let her go. We opened our fists as the ashes blew with the wind, watching as she flew away...forever.

I felt an ache growing in my chest that started coursing through my body. This was a painful moment, but I also felt a weird sense of relief because I knew she wasn't in pain anymore.

Maybe I was starting to realize little-by-little why she didn't want me to see her that way. I still hadn't come to the understanding of why she lied about my father, but there was still time to figure that part out.

After we spread my mother's ashes, and I had a face-to-face with her lover I knew nothing about, I started to get my writing itch. I said goodbye to Margot and Leo, and we parted ways.

I had brought my journal with me, but over the last few weeks, I couldn't find the will to pick it up. But now, I had all these feelings put in a box inside of me that needed an escape. I found a bench not far from the Pont des Arts bridge, where I reflected on my last journal entry—written just hours following my mother's passing, when I was at my secret spot overlooking the Boston Seaport. I hated what cancer did to her, to us. What it's taken from us, from me. Our small family unit was reduced to one, and I never felt so small.

Sitting on the bench, this journal entry started with: *Finally said goodbye to my mother today* and ended with: *Feed your soul with the things that make you happy.*

I hadn't heard from Pierre; I guess he took me saying *I would be in touch* to heart. But writing these last words out made me think of him for some reason, which was strange because all I should have been thinking about was putting my mother to rest.

I closed my journal, set my pen on top of it, and pushed it to the side of me on the bench. I picked up my phone, hovering over Pierre's number. There were so many things that could go wrong if I pursued him. He was Margot's son, and my time in Paris had an expiration date. Actually, not sure what could go right, but I also couldn't leave well enough alone. There was something about him that set my soul on fire, and my curiosity piqued. Maybe it was his stormy gray eyes, or his perfect dimples that shone through the light brown stubble lining his sharp jawline—most likely the charming French accent that did me in.

Whatever the reason, I didn't have to search far to find one for why I should finally text him after seeing him at *Frangipane*. Tapping on his contact, I hit the blue message bubble button and typed out:

Hey Pierre, it's Jules. I know it's been a few weeks, but I was wondering if I could finally take you up on your offer of showing me all Paris has to offer. Let me know what works for you.

After about two minutes of staring at the [...] waiting for his response, his finally popped up:

Hey Jules! Yes, of course. I would love to. How does tomorrow sound?

Tomorrow...Saturday...

I wasn't expecting him to answer so quickly, or be available that soon. First things first: I felt like the Eiffel Tower had to be on the top of my must-see list. Watching it from an airplane just didn't do it justice. Pierre agreed to meet me there at nine in the morning. I let Margot know I would be unavailable tomorrow, and that I think she knew the person well who was going to be taking up my time. She seemed to think it was a great idea.

And so did I, because I desperately wanted to feel anything else than how I was feeling today.

Pierre told me to meet him at the Trocadéro Platform, which he said is the most "spectaculaire" view of the Eiffel Tower. There was once a massive and beautiful palace named Palais du Trocadéro that was demolished to make way for Palais de Chaillot, which is what still stands in the square today.

I took the bridge that goes over the Pont d'Iéna to the Trocadéro. European architecture just hits differently. I honestly didn't even care to go to the top of the tower; I could just stand at the square staring at it all day. It helped being sunkissed by perfect 74-degree weather, as I was wearing a deep coral button down dress and black Steve Madden sandals. Sightseeing is horrible when sweat beads from every orifice.

When standing from the Trocadéro, the Eiffel Tower didn't appear as big as I expected, although it's more than 1,000-feet tall. Its intricate and puddled, wrought-iron lattice, pyramidal frame is divided into four parts separated by a floor. The second floor of the tower is made of four distinct pillars, but from there, they join in a single pylon, which rises vertically to the top. The Esplanade is basically the ground area below the Eiffel Tower where people wait and gather before going up the tower. The flooring is almost like smooth concrete with large blue square frames, some framed with a large taupe color with an eggshell-colored square filled in the middle.

Pierre said to meet him here early, so we could beat the crowd, and it would be easier to spot him—he was already there when I was walking up, standing on the top steps of Trocadéro Square, facing the Eiffel Tower, making it look like he was sitting under the middle of the tower. He was wearing a plain white tee and jeans, and brown boots, with a camera and strap hanging from his neck. He was a picturesque version of a young, dashing James Dean-type, who couldn't be any less attractive if he tried, and I practically drooled just looking at him. As I inched closer to him, I saw he was holding a bouquet of periwinkle peonies.

"You a photographer, too?" I teased, as I approached him.

Even though there were other people around—tourists invested in the Eiffel Tower—I was invested in him. Something everyone dreams about visiting, and I was finally here but infatuated with the man standing in front of me rather than the masterpiece that was more than 130 years old that towered behind him.

"As a matter of fact, I'm an amateur photographer." He stood before me and smiled crookedly.

His gray eyes glimmered in the rising sun, reflecting back an almost silver color that had me completely entranced.

"Touché." I smiled back, failing at hiding that I was blushing. "What's with the flowers?"

"Oh, well, these are for you," he grinned, handing me the bouquet. They were absolutely gorgeous, from the color to the way each flower burst through its layers. "I can't imagine how hard yesterday was for you, and I wanted to remind you of the beauty that surrounds you."

Pressing my lips together, I accepted the flowers. "Thank you, Pierre. That was a really sweet and thoughtful thing to do."

"You're welcome, Jules," he said with light in his eyes. A pause lingered between us before he asked, "Why don't you stand right here?" pointing to where he was standing, so the Eiffel Tower was right behind me.

I abided, assuming he was wanting to take a photo of me, and although I wasn't a fan of my photos, I would let him photograph me the entire day if he wanted to.

"How's this?" I asked, holding my arms up in the air on either side of me.

"Parfaite." He smiled, holding the camera up to his right eye. "Superbe...and I'm not talking about the tower behind you I've seen hundreds of times." He winked, totally unaware of the effect he was having on me—an all-encompassing feeling that made my heart beat faster and slower at the same time, focusing on him and only him.

If my translation serves me correctly, *superbe* means "stunning." Was I being swooned by an attractive Frenchman, who also happened to be my mother's best friend's son? Apparently I was—so much so, he was quickly making me forget why I was here in Paris in the first place.

But I couldn't forget nor did I really want to.

I felt like I was being pushed and pulled in different directions: should I be sad...or happy?

No, I should be happy, because Pierre makes me feel that way.

But, no, you should be sad because your mother just died.

Should I push away this best kind of distraction?

I had just said goodbye to my mother's ashes yesterday, but I felt like that was a weight lifted off me. But no matter how much I wanted to feel happiness, the sadness kept weighing me down. Maybe with the help of Pierre, I could actually see what my mother loved so much about her motherland. But it would take some convincing to pull me out of this state of conflicting emotions.

twelve

After Pierre snapped a few photos of me, we walked closer to the Eiffel Tower through the platform. This was the first day since my mother had passed away that I felt alive. That I felt there is hope for tomorrow, even though it wasn't there in my past.

It didn't take long for Pierre to dive into the French history that embodied where we stood. He explained to me that Trocadéro was named after an island in Spain known as Isla del Trocadero. This was the location of a famous battle won by France against Spanish rebellion forces in 1823. The French weren't fighting to take over Spain. They were actually fighting to help restore King Ferdinand VII's power. The result was King Ferdinand came back into power, and a beautiful park was built that would eventually provide the best Eiffel Tower photo opportunity.

He gave me a few quick facts about the Eiffel Tower's history, too—how old it is, how it was once yellow and was built to celebrate the centennial of the French Revolution, Alexandre Gustave Eiffel was the French civil engineer on the project, how it was the world's tallest structure for four decades. I obviously knew a lot of these facts he spewed per my mother, but it felt different hearing them said by a beautiful Frenchman himself. It was like everything he was saying I was hearing for the first time.

We stayed close to the Eiffel Tower and just walked around, starting with the Champ de Mars, a massive public park in Paris that forms a sort of runway to the Eiffel Tower. I saw a bike cruiser rental spot and suggested an idea I might later regret but thought would be fun at that moment.

"So...I'm well-aware I'm in a dress, but it's such a beautiful day, and those bikes look really fun. Would it take much convincing to partake in a bike ride?" I proposed, smiling coyly.

Pierre provided a light, closed-mouth grin before saying, "Absolutely not, chérie." He playfully nudged my shoulder with his and pointed his head toward the bike rental stand. "C'mon, let's do it," he said, grabbing my hand and pulling me toward the stand.

We rented two bikes and started biking side-by-side along the pathway. The bikes had cute little baskets, and we strolled along the endless, tree-lined pathway. Some of the trees' foliage was already turning slightly gold—just a hint of fall approaching—and it was absolutely beautiful. Fall was my favorite season after all.

We biked slowly, so we could still carry on conversation.

"So, how do you like being a journalist?" Pierre asked.

"How did you know? Do I just have annoying media girl dripping from my personality?" I joked as I paid close attention not to hit any pedestrians on the pathway.

"Of course not. I...how do you say it...grilled my mother about you...some," he said, and I smiled genuinely, looking over at him briefly before turning my head back to upright position.

He was so cute, and I was smitten that he inquired about me. I guess I piqued his interest enough to ask his mother about me, too.

I tried not to show my giddiness by simply answering his question. "I love it," I began. "I get to eat and drink at some of the most amazing restaurants in the country before anyone else does, get to discover others that are up-and-coming, and write about them. What's not to love?"

"Sounds like a dream job to me." He smiled, as we continued riding next to each other at a leisurely pace.

"How about you, what is it you do for work?" I inquired, realizing I didn't know much about him at all and hadn't had a chance to ask Margot, either.

"So, I'm actually in publishing...for Hachette Livre." This man with the bright smile, warm eyes, and cool disposition worked for one of the top book publishers in the world. I was beside myself realizing the emphatic and sudden attraction I had for him at this moment.

"Wow, so far, you haven't fallen short of amazing me," I mouthed before continuing. "What do you do for Hachette, how did you get into it? Tell me all the things. I know these are hefty questions for a bike ride, but the journalist in me must know...now." I let out a small awkward laugh.

But it's true; journalists are curious and impatient for information as it becomes available.

He let out a small laugh, too. "Sure thing. I'm an acquisition editor. So, I get to read raw manuscripts, and ultimately decide which ones get forwarded to the publisher. Not a bad setup," he explained. He said he always loved reading growing up and went to Oxford to study English and literature. Then, ended up moving back to Paris when he accepted a job as an associate editor, working his way up.

"I'm impressed, Pierre, really. Talk about dream jobs. Looks like we both are working ours." I grinned in admiration.

It was so easy to talk to Pierre. I didn't know if it was his carefree spirit, how we shared our love for words and culture, probably a lot to do with how attractive he is. Whatever it was, I was on a day-date that I didn't want to end.

We rode around for about thirty minutes before pointing out we were both famished.

We made a quick stop at a little café off the bike path to get a few sandwiches and some bottled waters and parked our bikes on a grassy area under a tree not far from the café to eat them. Whenever I was on any sort of date—the first few—I had this weird loss of appetite feeling. Almost as if there were literal butterflies fluttering in my stomach that made me not want to eat—as weird as that sounds. I think that, mixed with being self-conscious with how messy of an eater I can be, made it hard for me to eat in front of someone for the first time.

So, I picked at my sandwich, taking small bites here and there as Pierre and I eased back into conversation.

"You look really beautiful, by the way," Pierre said animatedly, while beaming a smile that made my world stop, along with his words. He took a bite of his sandwich, and I swear anything this man does—or says—is attractive, I'm sure of it.

"Thank you, Pierre. That's really sweet." I returned the smile, still picking at my sandwich. "You're looking handsome yourself."

He grinned before continuing to eat his sandwich, then after chewing he tapped his hand on my knee and asked, "Is everything okay? Are you not hungry?"

I looked down at my sandwich that was still pretty much whole. "I...uh...yea I'm good. I just have this thing about eating in front of people for the first time. Weird, I know, considering my job, but let's just say I've practiced taking really small and few bites." He nodded, and I changed the subject. "So, what's your relationship like with your mother?" I asked, knowing all too well that was a loaded question I wasn't sure he was ready to talk about, yet.

He finished chewing the bite he took before answering, "My mother is my rock. She has always been here for me, always pushed me to pursue my dreams, and never made me feel anything was impossible."

I smiled lightly at the words he reserved for Margot. At the same time, I had always felt the same about mine, despite how I was feeling about her now—betrayal, disappointment. No matter how those feelings made their way into my heart, I would always remember my mother for never faltering to be there for me when my father wasn't.

He didn't bring up what happened to his father, so I didn't pry—at least not this time. I figured he would talk about it when he was ready to.

After we ate, we continued biking around the park. He showed me a few museums along the path and shot a few photos of me on the bike. We rode back to the bike rental stand to return them, and I looked at my watch—it was already almost five p.m. Time escaped me today, yet I wasn't ready for the day to end, and apparently, neither was Pierre.

"How about the Seine River boat cruise? No better way to see the city, especially at sundown," he suggested, grinning from ear-to-ear.

It was refreshing, someone wanting to spend time with me like this and get to know me. I feel like most men I encountered just cared to get laid, so it was a nice change. I think that's why none of my previous flings ever lasted more than a month or so. I have always wanted more—a more serious relationship, but I think I was just waiting for the right guy to make time in my busy schedule for. Prior to Pierre, I didn't feel like anyone had been worth my time. And not only did I want him to take up my time, but I also couldn't deny this one. He had a hold over me I couldn't explain, but I was more than willing to find out.

"Let's do it." I smiled, as I waved my hand for him to lead the way.

Once again, he reached for my hand as he showed me the way. We walked to where the boat cruises were ported, which wasn't far, and got lucky with the next one departing at 5:40. As we waited for the tour boat to port, Pierre put his arm around me, and I let his warm and gentle touch linger over my shoulder.

"You know, I could get used to being your personal on-demand tour guide for the duration of your stay here in Paris," he said with a devilish but delicious grin.

There was a glint in his eyes, and I found myself lightly biting my bottom lip. "I might just have to take you up on that offer." I blushed, knowing all too well I could get used to it, too.

Other than the bartender who I thought was flirting with me at my birthday party, I honestly hadn't remembered how long it had been since I felt like someone was making a move on me—if that was what was happening here. I could have been wrong; it could be that Frenchmen just get handsy and are super friendly, but I highly doubted that was the case here—or, at least I hoped it wasn't. I liked Pierre, like *really* liked him. Being around him made me feel carefree, and it was just easy. No expectations, no trying to be someone that I wasn't—I was just existing with him.

When the tour boat ported and the previous tour's load of people filed out, Pierre reached for my hand again, interlocking my fingers with his this time, and we stepped onto the boat together, heading toward the bow. The feeling of his skin grazing mine had been electrifying, shooting pangs of fire through my entire body. I had no idea how a man I had met just a few weeks ago—and one date in—had made me feel this way—an effect no other man had ever had on me. Maybe I was just blind to it before or didn't allow myself to feel anything for anyone, and maybe I was more open to it now because I desperately wanted to feel anything than my heart breaking into a million pieces.

The sun was setting and colors of pink, orange and purple lit up the sky, as the reflection hit the Seine River. Small lights twinkled, lining the outside of the boat, and the Paris city lights reflected along the water. The sun completely set.

Once we got to the bow of the boat and picked a spot, Pierre dropped my hand slowly, standing close to the right of me—so close our shoulders were touching. The boat captain allowed ten minutes for all ticketed patrons to load before departing.

We headed out onto the water, the Eiffel Tower illuminated from a distance, and Pierre pointed toward the Louvre, the Musée d'Orsay, the Notre Dame Cathedral, as we passed them and floated along. They are all works of art, masterpieces to be marked not only in French history but around the world. Everything he showed me, although I'm sure were much different under the night sky than in the daylight, were only iconic photos I had seen in magazines—until now. Now, I got to experience what all the Paris rave is about, with an exceptionally handsome Frenchman. He was so passionate in the way he described each monument—in the way he smiled, the excitement in his voice, it was like he was telling someone about Paris for the first time, and it was the first time...for us.

After the tour boat came to a halt and docked, we filed off with the rest of the crowd. When we got off the short river boat cruise, I had realized we spent the whole day together, and he didn't ask about my mother even once. And I didn't think it was because he didn't care, but because he did. Maybe because he wanted me to remember Paris this way instead of why I was really here. And at least for today, he did just that.

I texted Bernard to pick me up by the Pont d'Iéna, where he dropped me off. Pierre waited with me until he got there.

"Thank you for today," I said, breaking the silence that hung in the brisk night air.

"You don't have to thank me, Jules. It was my absolute pleasure," he replied, gently grabbing my hand to plant a light kiss on the back of it.

The gesture was so small, but it had me swooning. All I could do was smile and bask in the way he made me feel—calm, cool, collected...and genuinely good. I was already looking forward to when I would see him again, and we hadn't even gone our separate ways, yet.

My eyes lingering on his for just a few moments longer made me wish I had the nerve to plant my lips on his. For a moment, I thought we were going to kiss, but instead, he pulled me in for a tight hug, kissed the top of my head, and flashed his infectious smile before waving me goodnight.

Pierre was changing my view on life right now, and I predicted changing his.

thirteen

Bernard dropped me off at the chalet at about 7:30 p.m. I changed into a knitted long sleeve and shorts sleeping set and slipped on a pair of socks that pulled up to my calves. I lit the logs in the fireplace and put a kettle of water on the stove to make some Twinings Earl Grey tea—nothing like bergamot to calm the mind as your nightcap. I had never been much of a drinker—other than being a mild wino.

Margot had texted me that she found some professional bakers to help out at *Frangipane*, which I didn't blame her. I didn't inherit my mother's love for baking and cooking—only eating—and I was just glad she was able to find some help, so I could get out of her way. I honestly didn't find joy in baking, or in running a bakery. I just wanted to feel closer to my mother, but I think there were other ways to do that than potentially destroying what she built from the ground up by burning it to ash. Margot made sure to also make it a point that she hoped I enjoyed my day of "sightseeing," with a wink face emoji.

Since Paris was now my oyster, seeing as I already got booted from my sad attempt at becoming an amateur baker, that meant I needed to find something else to do to occupy my time. Too bad Pierre was busy making a living, because he was the first thing that came to mind.

The tea kettle whistled, and I poured the steamed water over the bag of tea in a classic white mug. Taking the mug off the counter, I sat in the oversized beige accent chair adjacent to the fireplace. I set the mug on the side table next to me while the tea bag seeped in the water, pulled my feet up, and grabbed the throw blanket off the back of the chair, covering my legs with it. I watched as the fire embers went from red to almost black, sparks of orange flashing.

I reached for my phone to call Gen, although it was only a little after two p.m. in Boston, which meant she was at work. So, as expected, my call went to voicemail.

"Hey Gen, it's me. Had my sightseeing date with Pierre and just wanted to fill you in as I know you're dying to know the details. Anyway, I love you and miss you, and hope to hear from you soon." I ended the call and took a sip of my tea.

I walked up to my room to grab my journal then cozied back up in the chair by the fireplace. I received a text from Pierre making sure I made it back okay, and that he enjoyed today "very much."

Let's do it again...soon. Are you free tomorrow? was how it ended.

I was getting so excited about Pierre that I knew those feelings were outweighing my grieving ones. Although they were wholesome feelings that enveloped me much like this warm blanket, I still felt a tear within me. A tear caused by the push and pull of happiness and sadness.

As I studied my mug, I wondered if my mother sat in this same spot, with this same mug, thinking about Leo the way I was thinking about Pierre. Had she been *happy* here, even at the end?

I pulled back from my thoughts, trying to compartmentalize my mix of emotions.

I had just said goodbye to my mother's ashes a few days ago, and I didn't want to feel like I was erasing her death with a distraction, because that's exactly how I felt. But I also deserved to be happy, and I knew she would want that for me.

Pierre—someone who is nice, CHECK.

Pierre—someone who shows you around a foreign city, CHECK.

Pierre—someone who shows up with flowers when meeting you to show you around the city, CHECK.

What's not to fall for?

After realizing I had no cons on the list to pursue him further, I responded:

Absolutely. Since your mother fired me, my schedule is wide open lol.

I could almost hear his booming laugh as he replied:

Ha! I'm sure there is more truth to that. I have an idea, but it'll require us to start our day a bit earlier...

Why was he so damn charming? He was making me feel like a priority, like he was choosing me, and I desperately needed to feel that way these days—simply wanted.

I'm sure I can manage haha what time did you want to meet me?, I replied.

Fantastic. I'll pick you up at 8 a.m.?

Works for me, I confirmed.

Parfait. I'll see you in the a.m. Goodnight, Jules.

Wonderful, Goodnight, Pierre.

Taking another sip of my tea, I realized I was smiling. Pierre had an effect on me I couldn't necessarily describe. He had a weighted blanket of warmth kind-of-hold on me, one that I never wanted to take off. He made me feel calm and excited at the same time—something I didn't know was possible. I found myself staring blankly for a moment, just taking in how I was feeling. Like I was glowing from the inside out and couldn't remember when I smiled so much, even before my mother's death.

After I spent a minute or two gleaming over Pierre, I picked up my journal off the side table and opened it up to where I had left off. Writing in my journal became a several-times-a-day occurrence. Since I was on a leave of absence from the magazine, I had to get my fill some way, somehow.

Today was a good, no, a great day. I don't know how I could possibly have such a great day while grieving and missing my mother as much as I do. But Pierre gives me hope, excitement that I wouldn't have to live in this horrible grieving state forever, and he gives me much more than that. He gives me butterflies. He gives me peace. He gives me solace in knowing chivalry isn't dead. Looking forward to what tomorrow has in store.

My nightmares have turned into dreams since I met Pierre and journaling has also helped settle those disruptive feelings of grief and guilt. I was having less of them and not as frightening. Now I was looking forward to them rather than being afraid of them. However, they still made me feel like my mother was trying to tell me something—that there was even more truth she was hinting at in her mediocre letter.

My eyelids felt heavy, and the fire started to die down. After closing my journal and setting it on the side table, I pushed the blanket off of me and put the remainder of the fire out. I walked up the stairs and crawled into bed.

I drifted off to sleep, only for my reverie to be awakened by another dream—my mother was the star.

Her wavy brown hair that mirrored mine flowed past her shoulders. She was wearing a floral summer dress, and the light was so bright around her. She waved her fingers in and out and mouthed, "C,mon, my love." She was smiling, seeming eager for me to follow her. I grabbed onto her hand, and she pulled me into the light with her. I felt safe.

fourteen

My alarm blared at seven a.m.

I shuffled for my phone on the side table, nearly knocking the lamp over. Turning the alarm off, I reveled for a moment in how soft my body pillow was against my cheek as drool was leaking from the side of my mouth. After I came to my senses that I was back in my room in my bed, I turned on my back and wiped my face with my arm.

I now had less than an hour to make some coffee and get ready before Pierre was supposed to pick me up. Sliding my feet out of bed, I sat up and patted down my disheveled hair, taking a moment to wake up. I unplugged my phone from the charger and stood, padding down the stairs to make a cup of espresso—make that a double.

As I sipped on my espressos, I caught myself tapping my fingers on the island. Must have been a nervous tick. Nerves didn't even begin to describe what I was feeling right now, and surely the extra shot wasn't helping. I wasn't so sure I should be parading around Paris with Pierre like nothing happened. I was half-tempted to text him and tell him something came up, but then again, that wouldn't be fair to him. So, I decided to suck down my shame along with my espresso.

I headed back upstairs to quickly shower. With the towel still wrapped around my body, I brushed and blow-dried my hair with quivering hands. I tried to keep my nerves at bay when I finished with my hair to apply a little blush, concealer, and mascara but failed as I had to wipe away little specks of black that kept marking my eyelids. I threw on a sundress and sandals, eager to see where Pierre was taking me. I was allowing him to take the lead, which was honestly out of my comfort zone. After doing a onceover in the mirror, I grabbed my bag, headed down the stairs and out the front door with five minutes to spare.

He pulled up just two minutes later in a black 1960 Aston Martin DB4. Disclaimer: I knew nothing about cars, especially vintage classics, but he enlightened me on the car ride to the mysterious destination after I complimented it's pristine condition. I would have referred to it as "cute," but he described it as "elegant and sexy," which was a better fit to describe its beauty and allure. It had small, circular headlights along with the side mirrors, a shiny black exterior that looked like it was buffed often, and was the definition of classic elegance.

"The exterior is a lightweight Superleggera coupe body shell designed by Italian coachbuilder Carrozzeria Touring, a Tadek Marek 3.7-liter straight-six engine, and a speed and agility not seen in its predecessors, the DB4 is a class act in British carmaking," he said, sounding like a Google search passage. I'd have to admit, though, the way he talked about cars was sultry.

He lit up when he talked about it and explained it was a gift from his late father. I hadn't realized being fatherless was something we had in common; that drew me in further. It made me feel like maybe we would have more than a surface-level conversation. Did I want that? Was I ready to talk about the father I never knew but had always left a gap in my life? I also recognized I didn't know much about Margot at all—and apparently my own mother.

"Are you sure you weren't just speaking French to me?" I joked, as I played with the ends of my hair.

I had no idea what he was talking about, but I did know he was sexy talking about it.

He laughed, and it rattled me from where my thoughts were going. I didn't think I was funny, but I'd be lying if I said I wouldn't love making this man smile and laugh any day of the week.

Looking over at him and moving my sunglasses down my nose, I asked, "So, where *are* we going anyway?"

Pierre briefly looked over at me before shifting his gaze back to the ride, flashing a childlike grin. "Only the best châteaux in Loire Valley. It's called the Chateau de Chenonceau. It's about a three-hour drive."

Three-hour drive.

My mouth gaped open, but then I closed it, pushing my lips out. I was about to spend the next few hours riding in a car with a stranger. Sliding my sunglasses back up my nose to cover my eyes, I thought to myself, *what have I gotten myself into?*

"Is...that a problem?" he asked, breaking the brief silence.

"Nope, uh huh," I responded, shaking my head. "Not a problem at all."

"Bonne." He smiled, turning up the car radio a little bit. "Do you mind if I roll the windows down some? It's a beautiful ride to the valley, the hair-sweeping kind you probably took note of when watching those romantic comedy films women eat up." He threw his head back slightly, a loud laugh escaping from his throat.

"Excuse me, do I really look like the obsessed-with-roms type of girl?" I asked, offended but amused.

"Roms?" he questioned, trying to hold in a laugh and making me realize I left out the *-coms*. Palm to forehead moment.

Bursting out in laughter, I corrected myself. Sort of... "Roms...yea like you said, romance movies..." I said, trying to play my mistake cool.

"Ha! Gotcha, and no comment..."

The entrance to the castle was backed up by a long dirt pathway lined on both sides with thin strips of grass that boasted small shrubs and pink and red peony bushes. The ivory castle glistened under the morning sky in the distance, and I instantly appreciated Pierre for taking me here

Pierre grabbed his camera from the miniscule back seat and walked around the car to open the passenger side door for me, helping me out of the car. Headed down the pathway toward the castle, Pierre gave me another short history lesson. "This is probably my favorite chateau in the valley. It's based right over the Cher River, which we will see from one of the verandas. It was built in the 12th and 13th centuries and also known as the lady castle as it was under the ownership of many famous women in their day. The most significant part of its history was when King Henry the second gave it to Diane de Poitiers, which was a surprise to many, including his Queen Catherine de' Medici. It was Diane de Poitiers who commissioned the bridge over the river. After Henry passed, Catherine de'Medici took the castle from Diane de Poitiers and made it her residence, adding the immense and intricate gardens to the estate," he continued, pointing his hands toward the gardens as we proceeded on the path. "While the castle passed to many since that time, several other women came into ownership of this chateau, and it even served as a military hospital during WWI and was bombed in WWII."

Pierre clearly loved history, and I enjoyed learning more about French history from him. "You sure do know your stuff," I said, trying to kick the dust out of my sandals discreetly as we walked side by side. "This place is absolutely stunning, Pierre."

"You haven't seen anything, yet," he replied, stretching a big smile across his beautiful face.

Pierre inched closer and closer to me as we walked together, our shoulders brushing briefly. A part of me wanted him to reach for my hand as we got closer to the castle, but instead, he reached for something else.

Picking a peony off its bush, he turned to face me, stopping me abruptly in my tracks, just inches away from his face. "Did you know, generally speaking, a peony is symbolic of love, honor, happiness, wealth, romance, and *beauty*, and is traditionally given to someone special as an expression of joy?" he said, holding it out in front of me.

"Hmm, I did not," I said as heat rose from my neck to my face. His explanation took me back to when we went sightseeing, and he showed up with a bouquet of peonies. Maybe one day they would symbolize more than they do now.

I reached for the flower he held out for me, but he pulled it back. "Do me a favor? Take your sunglasses off."

Hesitantly obliging, I took them off slowly.

Staring into my eyes, I could feel his warm breath on me, causing a sensation below my navel. He tucked a strand of hair behind my ear, placing the flower there with it. Holding up his camera, he said, "Here, walk toward the castle."

He moved to the side of the pathway to allow room for me to walk. As I started inching closer to the castle, he said, "Look behind you at me now but keep your body facing the castle."

I turned my head and paused, flashing a grin at Pierre holding up his camera to take a photo of me.

After a few clicks, he jogged up the path to meet me.

"What was that for?" I offered a small smile to him, sunglasses still off, causing me to squint.

"No reason. You just looked too beautiful not to take another photo," he said, planting a small kiss on my forehead. He held out his hand and said, "C'mon, my love."

Just like in the dream of my mother.

Shaking away my feelings of déjà vu, I took his offered hand and followed him into the castle.

Pierre and I took a tour of the historic castle, going up on one of its verandas to see the river flow beneath it. As I looked onward to take in the views of the river, I felt a breeze wisp my hair behind me. That's when Pierre wrapped his arms around me and nestled his chin in the crook of my collarbone, pointing to all the dazzling gardens of flowers. In addition to the peonies, there was a garden of roses, too.

The rest of the afternoon with Pierre flew by. I found myself losing the concept of time when I was with him. I simply just enjoyed his company and could care less what the time was, just that I was spending it with him. For being practical strangers, our conversations flowed easily, and any silences were intentional.

After the tour, we drove back to Paris. I had fallen asleep and woke up to us pulling in front of the chalet, my hand gripped in his as I struggled to open my eyes.

"Are we...back already?" I asked sleepily.

"That we are." He kissed the back of my hand and said, "Let me walk you to the door." He walked over to the passenger side door to help me out again, and we hovered for a moment at the front door. "So, I had a really great time today."

"I did, too." I blushed. "Thank you so much for thinking of taking me there. I probably wouldn't have otherwise."

"The pleasure was all mine." His inflection turned more serious. "I'd like to ask you out on a *formal* dinner date...if you're interested."

The attention Pierre was paying me had me in a dreamy comatose state. I felt paralyzed trying to sort through my emotions of contentment and grief. I took a moment to contemplate ending it here with him or giving it a real shot.

I caught myself biting my lip and thinking of how guilty I felt to be so happy in these moments with Pierre when life should be so sad right now. I started shifting on my feet, because I wasn't sure if I should have been getting closer to a man when my time here was just a small blip.

After a few beats of being submerged deeply in the war in my mind, the latter won out. "Sure, I'd love that," I said, turning off the feud in my mind. "What day?"

"Wednesday night?" he offered.

"That works for me," I affirmed, really hoping our lips would finally meet.

But, Pierre just smiled in reply and kissed me on the cheek before telling me "goodnight."

Was that his move? What a tease. I could feel the anticipation ever-growing inside of me of wanting more from, of wanting to memorize the way his lips felt on mine, of wanting to pour all of these pent-up emotions and tension into this first kiss. But, for now, I accepted the build-up.

fifteen

I hadn't been on a real, dress up kind of classified date in at least six months. I had gotten bogged down with work, letting it consume me, because it was the one thing I had control over. Things tended to be so out of control for me, family-wise, I needed something that had stability—and for me that was work. So, this was a big deal.

When Wednesday rolled around, I did my usual closet roulette until I settled on a red, square-neck bandage dress, the hem hitting right above the knees, like I was dressing for revenge. Other than exclusive private chef selection outings for the magazine and occasional events here and there, I didn't have many opportunities to dress up, so I took full advantage once I got over my nerves deciding on what to wear.

Pierre picked me up at the chalet, and it took a moment to digest all that he was. He was wearing a light gray seersucker suit with a white tee under his blazer that made his eyes look a misty gray. His outfit complemented mine, and he didn't fixate on my chest or legs—his gaze was fixed on my eyes, and for the first time in a long time, I felt seen, recognized even.

"Wow...just wow, Jules. You look stunning." There was a want for me in his tone, and I couldn't help but smile.

"You clean up nicely yourself," I said, causing his lips to turn up into a smile I could look at all day.

He put his fist on his hip, leaving a loop under his arm to escort me to his car—chivalry wasn't dead.

"Shall we, belle?" He smiled, as I looped my arm through his.

He escorted me to the passenger seat of his Aston Martin. Pierre drove us to a small French fine dining restaurant on Rue Saint-Honoré in downtown Paris called Félix. It had valet parking, so we dropped the car off up front. He opened the passenger side door for me, and I stepped out onto the sidewalk with him, hand-in-hand.

The restaurant had a subtle romantic yet cozy vibe with low dim lighting, bookshelves on either side of the bar, French artwork on the lapis blue-colored walls, black and white railroad tile flooring, a mixture of cognac brown leather booths and tables with full-size leather accent chairs to match the booths, and light music filled the room; I recognized the song that was playing in the background—it was *Yellow* by Coldplay. *And your skin, oh yeah, your skin and bones. Turn into something beautiful.*

One of my favorite songs of all-time was playing in a restaurant...in France...with a man I had only just met. At that moment, I did believe the stars were shining for us tonight.

I continued humming along, as the hostess brought us to our table.

"You know this song?" Pierre asked. I guess the music wasn't loud enough to drown out my humming.

"Of course I do. Yes, Coldplay is technically a European band, but they are beloved in the U.S. as well," I replied matter-of-factly. Pierre grinned while pulling my chair out for me. It was yet another chivalrous gesture; chivalry being an afterthought I had stopped believing in—until now. "Have you ever been to the U.S.?" I asked him, sitting in the chair, as he stepped around the table to sit in his.

"No, I actually haven't. But should be on my list of things to do," he answered with a wink.

The hostess set the menus and wine list down in front of us, and as we sat across from each other, the brief silence and smiles felt comfortable. "Bonne soirée mes, chéris," she said, which translates to "enjoy your evening, darlings."

"You look absolutely stunning tonight by the way, Jules," Pierre reiterated, breaking the silence that lingered for only a moment.

"You already said that." I smiled, holding his gaze for just a moment longer.

"Well, you deserve to hear it more than once," he said with a more serious tone while his lips pinched at the corner of his mouth.

"So, shall we order a bottle of champagne? I've always wanted to have champagne in France," I said nervously, unsure of how to respond to his very flattering comment.

"Absolutely." His gaze moved down the wine list. "I wouldn't allow it any other way," he teased.

When the waitress came over to introduce herself, Pierre ordered us a bottle of Charles Ellsner Champagne and Fromage

Fort, basically fondue, to start. As a foodie, I wanted to try all the things, have all the courses, and appreciated that he took the liberty to order one of the restaurant's signature appetizers right away. Plus, I will take any food that has cheese on it, yes please.

After the waitress brought us our champagne flutes, we made a brief toast.

"To what comes next," I said, holding up my glass.

"To what comes next," he repeated, grinning and holding up his glass, clinking it with mine.

After we each took a sip, I reveled in its taste for a moment. Champagne in France was even more spectacular than I imagined—notes of crisp berries and citrus tingled on my tongue, lingering there.

Then, my interviewing commenced, while we waited for our appetizer to arrive. "So, you really intrigue me, Pierre. I must say, in a way that makes me want to know anything and everything about you," I said bluntly, making myself wonder how strong this champagne he ordered was.

"Is that so?" he asked amusingly.

Why did his smile and dimples have to be so damn beautiful? Scratch that, why did everything about him have to be so damn beautiful...

"It is so." I smiled, taking another sip of champagne while being aware of my surroundings, so I didn't drink it too fast. I didn't want to make a drunken fool of myself on our second date. "So, how has your week been so far? I'm curious what a day in the life of a book acquisition editor is like."

Interrupting us briefly, the waitress dropped our Fromage Fort off at the table with some cut up French baguette. "Bon appetit," she said before leaving us to it. We both dipped a piece of bread in the melted cheese, and I tried not to let my foodgasm show too much.

He took a sip of his champagne before continuing the conversation, "Well, on Sunday, I dove into a manuscript I finished today, that could be our next big hit." There was excitement in his voice, and it made me miss work—just a little.

"What's a *big hit* in this part of the world? Curious if it differs from what sells in the states," I asked, rubbing the bottom of my champagne flute.

"I must say, your guileless curiosity is intriguing." He smirked before continuing, "It does differ slightly. We publish a lot of historical fiction, culture, and philosophical books, and autobiographies and nonfiction. The imprint I work for is called Presse Millénaire—Millennial Press. But to answer your question, the manuscript is a nonfiction piece about a woman undergoing an identity crisis in her thirties."

"Isn't that all of us women, though? Even men, I suppose. What makes this one unique?" I was genuinely curious about the inside of a book publishing company.

He lightly laughed before answering, "Touché. But to me, this one is special because of her journey leading to said identity crisis. For example, she had a miscarriage, which led to her divorce and a string of mental health issues. It's a beautiful story of resilience, but I do think everyone's story and journey is *unique*."

"Touché." I nodded in understanding before taking another sip of my champagne, as he did as well, keeping his gaze on me.

The waitress came by our table shortly after to take our order. We both ordered the same thing per Pierre's recommendations: salade César to start, poisson du jour, which was a halibut filet with sautéed gnocchi and wilted spinach in a white wine garlic cream sauce. Doesn't seem like you could go wrong with that choice, so I gracefully allowed him to order for me, which was unusual. I didn't typically trust others to order for me when I knew so much about food.

Once the waitress walked off, he asked, "Do you want to be a food journalist forever? Or, are you open to other career avenues?"

"I agree with what you said about everyone's story and journey is unique, and to me, it's about telling stories through something that brings everyone together, and I truly believe food does that. It's not necessarily about nutrition, or even just my love for writing. These chefs, it's their livelihood, it's their art, and it's something people from all over the world come to see, come to enjoy. To me, there isn't anything like it." Maybe I missed work more than I thought.

"That's a really great reason to love and to continue what you're doing, Jules. You sound like you miss it. May I ask why you're staying in Paris for a few months?"

I beamed at his reply, as the waitress brought our salads over, then poured the rest of what was left in the first champagne bottle into our flutes, so we ordered another. I was going to need it to answer his question.

"I do miss work, actually. But I took a leave of absence to kind of figure things out here with my mom's estate and such. Plus I've never been to Paris and wanted to explore a little bit and just give myself some time to grieve, you know?" I purposefully left out the part about the letter—for now. I didn't want to have to explain all of that right now and put a damper on the mood with a serious conversation.

The waitress brought the second bottle of champagne over, popped the cork off, and filled our flutes.

Pierre smiled and responded, "I definitely can understand that. I mean, Paris has a lot to offer, and well there is one thing Boston doesn't have."

"And what's that?" I asked innocently.

"Me," he said straightforwardly, and the single confirmation made my breath hitch.

Smiling with my eyes, I said, "That's for certain." There was a tension lingering in the air and not the kind you didn't want to embrace.

When the waitress brought the rest of our food over, I was salivating—and it tasted as amazing as it looked.

"Pierre, you have really outdone yourself with these choices," I said, rolling my eyes while trying to contain the noise at the back of my throat from releasing—the sound I made whenever I was having a foodgasm.

He smirked, and I returned the smile. "I'm glad you're enjoying it. I was kind of worried with you being a food writer and all."

"Do you cook?" I asked.

"I do," he responded with confidence.

"I like a man who can cook—as you can already tell, food is the way to my heart," I joked.

"Maybe that'll be the next date. I'll cook for you," he said animatedly, leaning in closer with a small smile plastered on his face.

His offer sparked feelings of euphoria within me. This is a man who was already beginning to understand me, to understand food was the way to my heart—a man who can cook and was willing to cook *for* me.

I felt like I was slowly allowing myself to take these moments with him for what they were.

Trying not to show too much of my excitement to spare myself any embarrassment or desperation, I simply smiled and said, "I'd like that."

sixteen

The rest of the date went off without a hitch. Pierre was such a catch, and I found myself contemplating if there was a *catch*.

He dropped me back off at the chalet and walked me to the front door. We found ourselves back here, and this time, I wasn't letting him leave without a proper kiss, even if I had to make the move myself. The carnal tension between us grew thicker every second we were together, and it was becoming too hard to bear.

"I had a wonderful time tonight, Jules," he said with a beaming smile and glistening gray eyes I couldn't get enough of.

"So did I, Pierre." Blush and heat rose on my cheeks while anticipating a lean-in for a kiss, one I was desperately hoping for at this point.

"How about I come over on Friday night and cook you dinner?" He was smooth. I liked that he asked me out on the next date while on the current one instead of the usual "I'll *text* you and set something up."

"Sounds like a plan," I said, still wondering when that kiss was coming.

Without saying any more words, he smiled, tipping my chin up. I closed my eyes, leaning in farther until I felt his breath on mine, until our lips touched. They were so soft, and I finally felt that surge of magic I had been longing for since we met coursing through my body as our lips continued to move together as he strategically slipped his tongue into my mouth. I was up on my tiptoes as I threaded my hand around the back of his head, feeling his hair loosely gripped between my fingers. He pulled me into his frame, placing both his hands on my waist with a firm grip.

After a minute...or two...or what felt like an eternity, I pulled away from him so I could breathe, knowing all too well I'd still be out of breath from how he made me feel, opening my eyes to see the most beautiful, smiling man I had ever seen, like it was the first time.

"That was—" I started before he finished my thought.

"Mhmmm," he hummed, smile never faltering.

I gleamed, biting my lower lip in anticipation for more, but in due time I suppose.

We said our "goodnights," and I watched him walk to his car. I still enjoyed the back of him as much as the front. He opened the driver's side door before flashing me one more perfect Pierre smile, as I waved him off. I watched him drive off in his Aston Martin DB4 and shook my head as I walked inside the chalet.

I was already starting to fall for Pierre simply for who he is, and I felt like my heartstrings were being pulled in so many different directions, and it was overwhelming.

A call from Gen came in, shaking me from my thoughts.

"Gen! So happy to hear from you. I've missed you so much," I answered.

"Jules! Likewise, Doll. I'm so sorry I missed your call the other day. I've been SO slammed. Speaking of which, I only have a few minutes to catch up so give me your best brief," she said with eagerness.

"Well, your timing is impeccable. I just got back from my second date with Pierre. We went to dinner at this cute French bistro..." I trailed off before quickly being interrupted.

"SHUT THE FRONT DOOR. Well...how was it?!" she asked, surprised but enthusiastic.

"Everything you and I hoped it would be." Gen and I had often talked about what our dream men and life partners would be like. So far, what Pierre was showing me was that maybe they did exist after all.

"Ahhhh! I'm literally gushing. I'm so so happy for you, and you know I'm expecting a photo of him very soon."

"I think I can manage that."

I hope one day you will forgive me and see why it had to be this way, Juliette.

My mother's letter burned a hole in the desk drawer in my room.

It was almost halfway through September, and I was nowhere closer to finding out the undertones—or the truth—of that damn letter. I think in a way I was avoiding what I may find, and Pierre was sort of a vessel to do so.

Lying in bed staring at the drawer, I once again shook away the thoughts after looking at my phone and seeing it was Friday. That meant, Pierre was coming over tonight.

After going downstairs and making a cup of espresso, I took my seat in front of the fireplace and started writing in my brown, leather-bound journal that was soft from so many mornings holding it like this. It was a familiar friend by now, one I looked forward to sharing my days with—whether they were sad or happy. Every entry was a piece of me and reading back over my words made me feel more at home with myself.

Date with Pierre tonight. He offered to come over and make me dinner—I barely know him, and no other guy has ever done anything so thoughtful and sweet for me. I'm just following his lead, and that's so unlike me. I'm a journalist, a writer, so I only follow my own leads. But I like where this is going so far...

A knock sounded on the chalet's door promptly at seven p.m.

I opened the door to find a beaming Pierre, expressive gray eyes looking at me intently, making me want to get lost in the storm they were brewing. His smile was perfect, one I would love to cause every time I saw him.

He held up a bottle of Moët & Chandon, with a few canvas shopping bags hanging on either side of his shoulders. "I brought provisions." He smiled with prominent dimples.

"You come prepared, don't you? And how did you know this was my favorite champagne?" I said, lighting up.

"I didn't."

My eyebrows furrowed, shit-eating grin plastered on my face—and his. As cliché as it sounds, we didn't talk about our favorite wines on our first date. Moët & Chandon just happened to be his favorite mid-tier champagne, too.

I waved my hand, welcoming him inside the chalet. He followed me to the kitchen, setting the groceries and bottle of champagne down on the island.

"I've always thought this was a beautiful chalet," Pierre said, taking a look around with his eyes. "You inherited it from Esmée?"

"Yes. She left it to me in her will," I admitted, leaning my elbows on the counter. "I've been thinking of renting it out once I go back to Boston. I'm not sure what else to do with it. You've been here before?"

"That makes sense. Yes, a few times...toward the end," he hesitated to say.

Nodding, I embraced a brief moment of silence. Analyzing his features, I asked, "So, what's on the menu for tonight?"

Starting to pull the items from the grocery bags, he said, "I picked up fresh baked socca—a compliment of Mom's—to make rustic flatbreads with from scratch, pesto for the base, boursin and gruyère cheeses, caramelized onions, arugula, and prosciutto,"

"Sounds delicious." I smiled lightly. "How can I help?"

"Want to pour us glasses of champagne? Other than that, sit back and relax," he said, his lips turning up at the corners.

"Sure thing. I can do that." I opened the cupboard, pulling out two flutes, and popping the cork off the bottle.

I poured the bubbly liquid into the glasses, watching him move effortlessly around the kitchen, as if he had used it before. He sure knew his way around one, that's for sure.

"Merci, beauté," he said, raising his flute after I handed it to him. "Cheers."

"Cheers." I followed suit, clinking our glasses together.

I watched as he took a sip, his ashen eyes peering over the glass as they smiled at me.

Setting his glass down, he proceeded to whip up the pesto.

"Have you ever made pesto from scratch before?" he asked.

"No, I actually haven't. Side note, I may have inherited this chalet from my mother, but I did not inherit her wonderful chef skills. But clearly, you've inherited your mother's," I said with a hint of satisfaction. I was about to reap the benefits of that.

He laughed lightly before saying, "Pas de problème, chérie. I can teach you. C'est simple."

It was so damn charming when he spoke to me—period. Sure the French accent helped, but when he actually spoke to me in French, a strong desire for him swirled inside of me. It was just a foreign feeling to me—literally—one that grew the curiosity within me, wanting more.

"Step one, combine basil leaves, pine nuts or walnuts, and garlic in a food processor and process until very finely minced," he said, once again sounding like a Google search. "Step two, slowly dribble in oil and process more until the mixture is smooth. And step three, add the parmesan and process for just a moment longer, long enough to combine all the ingredients. Then, we put it in the refrigerator while the oven heats up and toss everything else on the flatbreads once it does. Voilà, see simple," he said, processing all the ingredients with ease, making me feel ashamed for ever buying store-bought pesto with how easily he whipped it up.

He preheated the oven to 200 degrees celsius (400 degrees fahrenheit) and took a butter knife to a stick of butter, letting it simmer on the skillet on the stove. He topped both our glasses off with more champagne, winked at me, and started chopping an onion, chef-style. The movements of the knife chopped so quickly and smoothly, his forearm muscles were twitching with every move, catching my eyes.

He had nice arms, and I'll admit, my mind drifted off thinking about what else he could do with his hands.

"Thank you," I mouthed, after he finished filling my glass up. Taking another sip, I said, "You must have watched your mother cook a lot when you were younger?"

"You could say that," he said, his back facing me, dropping the onions in the pan to caramelize. "How about you?"

"I definitely did. She had my bassinet in the kitchen for God's sake. When my father died...or left, rather, it was like she couldn't let me out of her sight." I could tell his body stiffened at my confusion, saying my father died first before switching to he *left*. But I continued, "I don't know, I guess I just didn't pick up on it enough when I was younger, then when she moved back here when

I was eighteen, it was like all of it was lost on me. I was upset that she never taught me French, either."

I hadn't known Pierre for very long, but I found myself opening up to him sooner than I usually did. I didn't know if it was because I missed my mother, and he just reminded me of home—how she was home for me—and now being back where she last was, I couldn't help but feel vulnerable.

He turned to face me, leaning in closer. Placing a hand over the top of mine, his eyes bore into me, like he was trying to deep dive into my soul, he said, "Jules, I'm sorry to hear about your father—and that you can't cook, or speak the greatest romance language in the world," he said to lighten the mood, an innocent grin forming on his lips.

He didn't pry about my mix-up. Pierre made me want to talk about the neglected parts of me, though, which included the father I didn't have a full history on. Just a few scraps I was still piecing together myself. I didn't even know if I would have a clear picture in the end, which poked at my heart a little bit.

I choked a little on the champagne I had just swallowed before setting my glass down.

Locking my eyes with his, I said, "Oh, you think you're funny, do you? Since you speak the greatest romance language?"

"Mhhmm..." he sounded, as the oven timer dinged.

"Saved by the bell," I joked.

Pierre gave me another wink before he slid his hand off of mine and finished caramelizing the onions, turning the stovetop burner off, and laying out the two flatbreads. He pulled the pesto from the fridge and spread it across each of the flatbreads. He then spread boursin cheese on them and freshly grated gruyère cheese, the caramelized onions, arugula, and pieces of prosciutto.

"Looks delicious, Pierre," I said, as I was practically drooling.

I couldn't wait to try Margot's homemade flatbreads. Just like my mother, everything she made was literally golden.

"Why thank you, mademoiselle," he said, as he carefully placed each flatbread in the oven. "We just leave them there for about fifteen minutes, and then we feast."

"Perfetta," I said, making a chef's kiss gesture.

He laughed out loud. "Do you mean, *parfaite*?"

I shook my head in embarrassment, my cheeks surely blushing in this palm-to-forehead moment. "Yes, thank you for the correction, Mr. Editor," I deadpanned, as he continued laughing lightly. I believed I spoke in Italian, not French.

After the flatbreads were finished cooking, we sliced them into squares on a large wooden cutting board. We took the board, a few appetizer plates, what was left of the bottle of champagne, and our flutes to the living room, setting everything on the oversized ottoman in front of the fireplace that I had graciously lit, for an ambience effect, before Pierre came over. I sat on one side of the ottoman, and he made sure to sit as close to me as possible, with just enough room his elbow could bend while he ate. Being so close to him caused an arousal to ignite inside of me.

"Ladies first," he said, gesturing toward the flatbreads.

Shaking my thoughts away, I smiled as I scooped a few pieces onto one of the plates and took a bite. It was only date two, and I was already having another orgasm—a foodgasm, that is. A groan deep in the throat that desperately wanted to escape, much like an actual sexual orgasm...only while eating.

"Pierre, my goodness, this is really delicious. Thank you so much," I said, finishing that piece off.

He had waited patiently for me to savor it before he dug in. "My pleasure, amour," he said, smiling in satisfaction that I was enjoying the food he made. "I'm glad you enjoy it."

As he slipped a few pieces of flatbread on his plate, he said, "I didn't mean to make light of your father leaving in the kitchen, by the way. I know it's been hard with your mother passing away, and I just wanted to cheer you up. Do you want to talk about him, though? I'm all ears."

He took a bite of his flatbread, looking at me intently with more questions behind those dark eyes of his than what he was saying with his mouth.

I took a large gulp of my champagne before answering him, "Can we come back to that?"

"Of course," he said, leaning his back into the couch, throwing an arm casually around me as he stared between me and the fire. He took a sip of his champagne with his free hand and acted like he had all the time in the world to tend to me.

I made sure to take my time warming up to him as I didn't feel like divulging all my dirty laundry at once. I watched as the fire danced in his eyes, hoping he would kiss me already, kiss away all the shame I was feeling, mooring me where we sat.

But instead, he placed the hand that was gripped around my shoulder to my ear, allowing my head to rest on his shoulder for a moment. Closing my eyes, I took a deep breath, accepting this moment for what it was: harbored on his island, not mine.

Maybe Pierre was becoming my anchor in this storm. He made me feel calm when everything around me felt chaotic.

seventeen

Pierre and I had finished off the flatbreads and the bottle of wine, as we dove into conversations I didn't think you could have with an almost-stranger. He was a great listener, and I found myself wanting to give him plenty to listen to.

I talked on and on about how Gen and I are best friends, and she's been my rock through every hardship, how my life would have been different had my father not left, about our careers, what our family goals were. He also opened up about how his father died when he was a teenager, in a "silly" skiing accident, and Margot never remarried, how she, too, had been discreet about any relationships she's had, which led to me venting about my mother's secret boyfriend, Leo.

"So...it's kind of *complicated*," I said, now feeling comfortable enough to share more with Pierre—a few glasses of champagne in. "For twenty-seven years, I believed my father had died when I was three years old, because that's what my mother told me. And she never told me how, just that he died. But when she died, she had written me a letter that said he actually didn't die. He took off, and she didn't want me to grow up knowing he didn't *want* me. She thought it would be easier that way."

"Easier for you...or for her?" This was a question I had been considering since I read that letter.

"You know, I'm still trying to figure that out." And I was. "Plus, I found out she was dating this guy..."

I had been lied to for most of my life, and I didn't know what hurt more—that my father actually left on his own free will, or that my mother knew about it and made me believe this entire time that he was dead. And every fiber in my being needed to find out why. But in the meantime, I was still just trying to process it all.

"That's a lot of weight to carry, Jules," he said earnestly, as he rested his elbow on the couch, his fist to his cheek, furrowing his eyebrows as he looked at me attentively. "As someone who has lost a father, by death, I couldn't imagine also losing my mother. You lost yours in such a slow and painful way, and to come here and find out the truth about your father, that he chose to not be in your life, I can't imagine how you're feeling right now. His words sent barbs through my heart, as he continued. "You're a beautiful person, and honestly, it should be the greatest mistake of your father's life for walking out on you like that."

I couldn't force my tears to stay put as they freely fell from my eyes. Pierre cradled either side of my face and gently wiped them away with his thumbs. He tipped my chin up, our eyes meeting, his filled with sadness for me as they formed a squint.

"Thank you for the kind words, Pierre. Really, it means a lot. But I must also correct you. For me, my mother's death wasn't...*slow.*"

He knitted his eyebrows in confusion. "What do you mean? She had cancer, right—"

I cut him off, "Yes, she did. But I didn't know she was dying until Margot called me to tell me she had died. It was at my thirtieth birthday party." His mouth fell open, like he wanted to say something but couldn't find the words, so I continued, "There's really nothing you can say. I've been going through a lot lately, trying to figure how all of this could turn to shit so quickly, and I'm honestly coming up blank. When you had asked why I decided to take a leave of absence from work, I wasn't 100% honest with you. This was why...I needed more answers. Answers for why my mom didn't tell me she was dying, why she lied about my father, why I didn't know about her and Leo. Then I met you, and for a little bit, I kind of forgot why I was here. And I liked...that I did."

"Jules, I'm so sorry," he said, pity lacing his tone. "I really have no idea what to say. I guess...maybe," he struggled to find the words before gathering his thoughts, "are you still looking for answers?"

Maybe Pierre could give some outside perspective on what I should do: do I go looking for my father or not?

"Well, after spreading my mother's ashes, I realized I could respect the fact that she didn't want me to see her *that* way, as she put it. As for my father, no I haven't."

"I don't think you should stop looking." His words were so honest, and I found myself hanging onto them.

"I've been racking my brain, trying to figure out my next step. Do I let it go and just grieve? Or, do I go searching for answers I might not get, sending me into a further tailspin. What would you do?" I asked him as he continued peering into my soul.

"I'd go searching."

His words had me contemplating everything that had unfolded. Before me was a man I had just met. The same one who was allowing me to forget about all the hurt I had when I came here and all the hurt I found after arriving, and was now pushing me to get the closure I needed. "We should start with my mother."

There was a lot to unpack in our lives. Things were coming out of me like never before, and I wanted nothing more than to explore every inch of who Pierre was—emotionally...and physically.

It was almost midnight when I walked him to the front porch to say our goodbyes for the night.

I leaned against the doorframe and took a moment to look up into his beautiful gray eyes. I saw a mystery I wanted to unfold in them, but I also spotted a glint of desire.

"Thank you again for the flatbreads and champagne. That was really sweet of you to come over...and to let me talk your ears off," I said, softly smiling.

"Jules, you don't have to thank me, really. I can't think of anything else I would have rather been doing." He smiled gently, as I nodded.

"Me neither, Pierre." We shared another comforting silent moment, staring at one another, before he placed his hands on my hips, pulling me so close to him I could feel my racing heart pumping on his chest muscles; the chest muscles I savagely wanted to expose so I could run my hands over them.

His hands found my face, leaning down to press his lips on mine.

Embracing the kiss deeper, I twisted the hem of his shirt, kissing him like I needed him, right then and there.

He raked his fingers through my hair, as his tongue moved in and out of my mouth. Breaking free from our grips, he pulled away, staring at me intently, his mouth slightly open and breathing heavy. Ignoring the possibility of where this could have ended up—back inside—he said, "So, I'd love to take you somewhere tomorrow. You free?"

Trying to catch my labored breathing, I responded, "Yeah...sure, I'd love to. I was actually going to see if your mother was at Frangipane in the morning and catch up with her, especially after your comment about starting with her, you know for some more answers. Want to just meet there a little after I talk with her?" I asked, excited to see him again, but at the same time, dreading any further conversations with Margot about my mother and her past—our past.

"Sounds like a plan. I'll be there at eleven," he said, planting a small kiss on my forehead. "You sure you don't want help or support when you talk to her? I know it's not my place, but I'd be happy to...if you needed me."

Gushing, I said, "I appreciate the offer, but I think I should handle this alone, for the time being. But I'll see you tomorrow."

"You got it. Goodnight, Jules," he said, grinning ear-to-ear.

"Goodnight, Pierre." I offered a one-sided smile.

He turned to walk toward his car, and just a few feet in, I said, "Oh, hey, do I get any hint as to what we'll be doing tomorrow? Want to make sure I'm dressed appropriately."

"Just dress comfortably." He winked before slipping into the driver's seat.

Even as he drove off, I lingered on the porch for a few moments, finding myself still smiling and wanting to bask in his presence—in the sense of still feeling him around me, that's how his warmth felt.

This man had me on my toes, physically and metaphorically.

As I turned to walk inside, the feeling of dread grew in the pit of my stomach. I had no idea what I was going to ask Margot, nor did I even know if my mother told her much, anyway.

All I knew was that there were answers waiting for me—somewhere. The question was: who did they lie with?

eighteen

There was a sweetness about doing nothing—about having absolutely nowhere to be.

As an American, we are taught that work comes first. We work so hard we burn ourselves out to the point of no return, to the point of lack of enjoyment for life in general.

So, for a few moments, a few months rather, I wanted to be *un-American.*

I feel like most people settle for misery, because they are afraid of change. Last night when Pierre left, I couldn't go to sleep—probably a mix of being eager to see him the next day and not being able to wrap my head around my mother being gone, yet, and having to approach Margot—so I turned on the TV. *Eat, Pray, Love* was on—one of my favorite books made into a movie—and something the main character said, who is based on a real journalist, Elizabeth Gilbert, stuck with me: "Ruin is the road to transformation."

Sometimes people have to be completely destroyed, completely torn down—mentally, physically, emotionally—before they change...before they have no choice but to change. I wasn't sure what I was searching for upon my arrival to Paris, but what I did know was that I was completely destroyed, completely torn down, mentally, physically, emotionally. I was searching for answers for why my mother died without telling me, why my father abandoned me, why she never told me, who Leo was, and for love I may never find. Sometimes you have to face the worst—and the most painful thing—in order to rebuild yourself. I wondered what my mother had to face to rebuild herself. I wondered if her road to transformation had been cut short.

After waking up, I stared at myself in the mirror; I couldn't say I recognized myself.

No matter how hard I tried I couldn't shake the ruminating thoughts from my mind. And it showed in every line, every wrinkle, every shade of black in my brown eyes. But I needed to get dressed to see Margot at Frangipane—and meet her son who was taking me on some sort of surprise rendezvous. So, like I had done every day, I pushed the feelings and thoughts down deep, that is, until they came up again.

Just dress comfortably. What does that even mean, really? I had no idea where Pierre was taking me, and I didn't want to dress down but not too done up, either. I took "comfortably" at face value and threw on a pair of black active leggings, a white t-shirt, and my tennis shoes. After I was done getting dressed, I headed out the door, excited for what the day could bring while also dreading the fact I eventually needed to face my past.

Margot said she would be helping out at Frangipane today, and I hadn't seen her since I had been on almost three dates with her son. I reached for the doorknob of the powder blue door, the bell above dinging, indicating I had stepped inside. Margot was putting pastries in the display case and looked up when she heard the bell, beaming a flawless and radiant smile—this must be where Pierre got his.

"Gentille fille, how are you? So good to see you," she said, putting her hands in a prayer position and bringing them to her lips for a brief moment before making her way toward me.

She kissed both my cheeks before embracing me in a warm and firm hug.

"Salut, Margot," I said, smiling and pulling out of the hug. "I'm doing alright, all things considered. It's good to see you, too. How have things been around here?"

"Oh good, but you know I don't want to talk about that. I'd love to hear more about how my handsome boy is as your tour guide," she said with a wink, making me blush. "You know, he can't stop talking about you! I told him I have to work, and so does he." She laughed.

That revelation made my heart smile. Now I definitely knew Pierre hadn't just been my *tour guide*. And how was I supposed to bring up anything serious with these comments? She seemed so happy.

"I mean, I don't want to kiss and tell, but I really like him, Margot. Is it okay that we have been spending time together?" I asked with a sense of asking her for permission. I didn't want it to be weird between us.

"Are you kidding? Of course I don't mind, darling. I know he will be in good hands with you." She smiled, granting me the permission I needed to move forward with Pierre. I looked down on the floor unsure of what to say next. Margot put her hands on my shoulders. "Hey, Jules, you okay, sweetie?"

Steeling myself, I just went for it. "No, actually, Margot, I need to ask you something," I trailed off.

"Of course, ask away," she said, furrowed brows atop her usually well-lit brown eyes.

"I don't know how to ask this, so I'm just going to do my best," I started. "I was wondering if you knew anything about my mother lying about my father dying...that he actually left..."

Margot's eyes grew wider, she pursed her lips, and something else I couldn't place appeared on her face, almost as if she was expecting me to ask but was hoping I wasn't going to. "I...um...Jules, I'm sorry," she stumbled over her words. "I wish I could help, but I honestly don't know anything about that."

I wasn't sure if I believed her, so I pressed, "You're telling me your *best* friend never let you in on her dirty little secrets?" I instantly recognized I was coming off as rude, but I honestly had zero fucks to give at this point. I was so angry and frustrated, and maybe didn't realize it at the moment, that all my pent up anger and frustrations were directed toward the wrong person, almost like I just needed to point the flood of emotions at something, anything.

"Jules, look, I don't know what to say—"

I cut her off, "How about Leo? Do you have nothing to say about that either?"

Saved by the bell. Some sort of timer was going off in the background, interrupting our conversation.

"Oh, shoot, the croissants are done. Give me a moment?" Before I could answer, she scurried away to tend to the pastries while I stood, wanting more than what I got.

Was there more she wasn't telling me?

As I stood in the bakery, flabbergasted that damned croissants broke up my investigation, I heard another bell—the bakery door opening.

I turned to see Pierre. Glancing quickly at my watch, he was picking me up promptly at eleven. I must have arrived later than I wanted to, or time flew by.

He beamed as the door shut softly behind him. Walking toward me, he said, "It's good to see you." He pulled me in for a hug, squeezing a little tighter, my cheek to his chest as he laid his chin on the top of my head.

"Oh, hi, son. I didn't hear you come in," Margot said, coming out of the kitchen carrying a tray of fresh-baked croissants, breaking up our moment. Setting them down on the counter, she took my place by hugging her son, kissing him on each cheek. "Where are you two off to?"

I took notice that I had been spot on with what I was wearing. Pierre was dressed in a sweat-wicking shirt, active shorts, and tennis shoes as well. "Yes, where *are* we going?" I asked.

"If I tell ya, I'll have to kill ya." He smiled and then winked. "Sorry we can't stay long, mom, but we should get going. You ready to go, Jules?" Pierre said, and I was thankful we wouldn't be staying long.

I didn't want to ruin a perfectly good day by furthering my conversation with Margot in front of Pierre. "Yes, let's do it," I said, as he reached for my hand to lead me to the exit.

He waved at Margot. "Bye, Mom. It was good to see you, too."

"Margot," I said, nodding.

"Have fun you two," Margot said, waving us out the door with a crooked smile. My questions seemed to have shaken her up a little bit.

Once we exited the bakery, I asked again, "So, are you going to tell me where we are headed, yet?"

Pierre opened the passenger door for me, and I wondered if this gesture was something he was doing just at the beginning of us dating, or if he really did have as good of manners as he was showing this early on.

"You'll see." He smirked as he slid into the driver's seat, starting his Aston Martin, and pulling onto the cobblestone road.

We headed outside of Paris, up a winding road leading to the hills. We exchanged glances at each other, ones filled with adoration, as soft pop music filled the background. The foliage was absolutely breathtaking, colors of gold turning into red, like a watercolor painting. I was just enjoying the ride, embraced in Pierre's company, just the thought of him existing while bringing light into my life I didn't know I needed at a time of darkness. The air slipped through the cracks in my fingers as we drove, and I felt both the strength of the wind and yet how soft it was. Both reminding me of the man sitting beside me, stealing glances as often as the winding road would allow. I had to shake away the conversation I started to have with Margot, so it wouldn't rub off on my time with Pierre, but something about it was off-putting.

We drove to the top of a hill, parking the car in a secluded overlook that afforded a stunning view of Paris.

"We're going hiking?" I asked excitedly. I loved hiking and didn't get to do much of it in Boston. The idea took me by surprise, but I loved it.

He smiled. "That we are. But first, this view of the city is worth seeing before we do.".

Getting out of the car and walking around to open my door, he held out his hand, and we made our way toward the overlook. There was surprisingly no one else there, just the two of us, breathing in and out the same fall air. He gently dropped my hand, placing his arm around my shoulders, and I placed an arm around his waist, as we looked onward, soaking in the grandiose view that lay before our eyes.

I briefly closed mine as I felt a breeze sweep through. Other than that, all I felt was Pierre's summery embrace, wrapping me in that warm blanket that gave me peace. His arms felt light around just like he made me feel on the inside.

"Pierre, this is absolutely beautiful. Do you come here often?" I asked, soaking in the view.

"I do. This is where I come when I need to *think*, clear my head. I came here after my father died, and I don't know, ever since it's just been a place that's given me peace." After he said that, I thought back to my quiet place overlooking the Boston Seaport back home. The place I returned to when I needed solace, the place I went after my mother died.

Pierre and I were connected by the way our souls saw the world, and at that moment, I realized why falling for this beautiful man was so easy.

Everyone needed a place like this, and when you feel like you can share that place with someone else, you would think it would threaten your refuge, but that wasn't the case—at least not here, not with us. I wondered what that meant to Pierre.

"Well, thank you for taking me here, for sharing it with me," I said with gentleness in my voice.

He leaned in and spoke directly into my ear, sending shivers skating across my skin. "It is a special place, and you're a special woman, Jules."

I looked up at him with eyes starting to fill with water—not because I was sad, but because Pierre had a way of replacing my pain and grief with an overwhelming amount of ecstasy and comfort. I turned to look at him then leaned in, closing my eyes and pressing my lips to his.

He smelled of sandalwood and earth, physically and emotionally grounding me right where we stood. His lips were soft and warm as they moved with mine, and I was convinced it wasn't my mother's death—or her letter—that brought me to Paris. Maybe the universe had other plans for me that didn't involve death, abandonment, or grief. Maybe it planned to bring me something I needed for once. Maybe he was going to be the one who saved me.

The hike was short, only two miles long, but it gave us the opportunity to get to know one another a little better: what he remembered about his father, what it was like growing up without one, what was growing up like with our mothers.

Pierre parked in front of the chalet after the hike, and I invited him inside. Apparently, he had a change of clothes in his trunk anyway. How convenient.

We walked past the threshold of the chalet, but this time it felt different. I could feel the tension in the air, the kind of tension you didn't want to hold back from but rather embrace. I wanted him to unravel me. Pierre dropped his bag on the living room floor and locked eyes with me. The seconds ticked on and the silence we shared was deafening.

He was the first to break the silence. "I meant what I said, Jules. I do think you're special," he said as he took a step closer.

"I believe you. But I'm curious, what makes me so special? I feel like you could have anyone, so why me?" I asked, bracing myself for the answer.

A sense of insecurity had washed over me with how fast I was falling for him. We hadn't known each other but for a few weeks. My mind flashed back to the moments we had already shared, though, and I found something redeeming in them, a redemption I couldn't ignore.

Stepping even closer, so we were face-to-face, he professed, "Maybe I could have anyone, but that doesn't mean I *want* any of them. I want you," he said, stopping my heart before he continued. "I want you, because you know what you want. I want you, because you're so beautiful, and you don't even know it. I want you, because you make me smile, you make me feel alive. Just being here with you now gives me a comfort I didn't know I needed. I want you, because you see the world in a way that's so you...in the way I also see it...and I can't even explain it. Despite all you have been through, all you are going through now, you find a way to enjoy the little things."

"That's a damn good answer. Pierre, I—"

Before I could finish telling him how he made me feel, too, he inched closer to me, tipping my chin up and gently pressed his lips to mine.

His warmth, his touch wholly enfolded me.

Placing my hand on the back of his neck, I pulled him in closer. The feeling of his lips on mine, of his hands gripped on my waist as the world fell away with every movement of our lips together was intoxicating. I pulled away from him, and without any words I took hold of his hand, leading him upstairs. I turned on the faucet to the shower in my ensuite, placing a hand under the lukewarm water until it was steaming.

"Jules...are you sure?" he asked in understanding of what I wanted at this moment.

I was tired of living life afraid of the unknown. I was thirty years old, and other than my career and Gen, I honestly didn't know what I was living for. I kept making excuses, reasons not to find out. So, I took this moment with Pierre for what it was and rolled with it. I was happy being around him, with him in the present. And to me, at that moment, all that mattered was the present.

"Pierre, you understand me in a way no other man has. You've been supportive during this time of grief for me. For just this moment, I don't want to think. I just want to continue feeling what I feel when I'm with you without holding back. You don't have to worry about taking advantage of me. So, yes, I'm sure," I said, and he followed with a nod. He was not only the best kind of distraction for me but the choice I would choose over and over again.

I grabbed the end of his shirt, and slowly pulled it up over his head. Then he did the same to mine, his fingers skimming my ribs, the sides of my breasts, and up my arms. Before I knew it, the pile of our clothes lay on the floor, and I stepped into the steaming shower, Pierre following behind me. The warm water pouring down on me felt as if it was washing me clean, hearing it patter against the tiles was clearing my mind.

I was marred by the grief of my mother, finding out about how my father left me, that she lied, the feeling his mother might have been in on it, but all that mattered right now was this moment with Pierre.

As I faced the wall with the shower head, water streaming down my face as I closed my eyes, he wrapped his arms around me, the muscles in his forearms prominent as I placed mine over his. He started planting kisses along my neck and shoulder, and we lingered like this for a moment.

My eyes fluttered open as I felt him harden behind me, and I dropped my hands and his from my torso. Turning around to face him, I saw the gray storm of desire brewing in his eyes. My gaze moved down to his biceps, then his abs, sculpted to perfection, taking all of him in and lightly gasping for air as he literally took my breath away.

His eyes traveled over my body before he said just above a whisper, "You're so beautiful, Jules. Every inch of you."

I was too caught up in his words to formulate any type of response at this moment.

He pulled me into him, turning me around so my back was up against the shower wall now, opposite of the shower head. He placed a hand on either side of my head as my back pressed into the wall farther. His eyes never leaving mine, his hands traveled down the sides of my body, scooping me up, my legs wrapping around his frame as he held me up against the wall, his body pressing into mine. I ran my hands through his hair, placing my lips on his again.

I waffled back and forth in my mind. Even though I already told him I wanted to do this, there was a part of me that felt like I was trying to mask the other emotions I was feeling with a physical connection. But Pierre was so much more to me than that, however, I still questioned myself. "Are you sure we should do this? Maybe...we should wait?" I searched his face for answers, even though I knew I was too invested to move forward with him to stop now.

"I'm not going to lie. It would be hard for me," he said in between heavy breathing. "But, of course, if you want to stop, I will respect that, respect you."

Although he was pinning me to the wall with his abdomen, he held me gently, awaiting my permission to enter me. The decision shouldn't have been one up for debate any further, and I didn't want it to be at this point.

Nodding yes, I pressed his face to mine, passionately kissing him like there was no tomorrow.

With one more movement, he was crashing into me, possessing every fiber in my being. I titled my head back as the warm water pummeled down on us, feeling every inch of him move inside of me.

Right now, he was all that mattered.

nineteen

I woke up to a beautiful Pierre, whose head was lying on my chest, his arm wrapped around my middle. Trying not to wake him up, I reached my hand over to the nightstand where my phone was. It was six a.m.

Carefully slipping out of Pierre's embrace, I unplugged my phone from the charger, threw on my robe, and paused for a moment to look at Pierre sleeping peacefully. Opening up my phone's camera, I snapped a quick photo of him before heading down the stairs to make some coffee.

As it was dripping, I decided to dial Gen to keep her updated on the Pierre situation. She was likely on her lunch break, and this was the type of news that I knew she would be dying to hear.

"Hi love, how are you?!" she answered excitedly.

"Hey girl, I've missed you! I'm doing alright, all considering," I said, not jumping into why I called immediately. "How are you? How's work?"

Putting her on speaker and laying the phone on the counter, I pulled out a small espresso cup and saucer and poured the espresso into the cup.

"Oh, you know, all the same. Nothing new there, but I have a feeling there's something new with you..." she trailed off, and I should have known she knew me too well to tiptoe around the reason I called her.

"You caught me." I laughed before continuing, "Well, there is a specific reason I am calling you right this minute...at six in the morning," I said, taking a seat on a barstool at the kitchen island.

"Spill it," she said bluntly.

"There may or may not be a gorgeous Frenchman sleeping in my bed right now..." I said just above a whisper so she could hear me but hopefully Pierre couldn't.

"SHUT THE FRONT DOOR! Give me all the deets," she said, and I knew I wouldn't get off that easy.

"Well, you know, it started off with the sightseeing, then he came over and made me dinner, and he took me to this secluded overlook with the prettiest view of Paris, that he said he goes to when he wants to be alone, took me to Loire Valley and literally picked a flower for me while we were walking up to this magnificent castle...and I don't know, one thing led to another, and you know..."

"Omg, sounds like a dream love. Are you...falling for him?" Gen was never one to beat around the bush.

"Yea, I think I am." It was hard to say these words with all of the conflicting feelings I had—falling in love and grieving my mother along with the betrayal that came with that. But, I'd be lying if I said there wasn't a wholehearted truth to them.

Gen must have sensed the angst in my voice, because she replied, "You know it's okay to be...happy, right?"

Taking a sip of my coffee, I weighed her words for a moment. "Is it, Gen? I mean, my mother just died, and all the stuff with her lying. I just don't know how to *feel* right now to be completely honest," I said, taking a small breath before I continued. "And with an even more recent turn of events, I have a feeling Margot knows more about my past than I do..."

"Jules, you have been through SO much," she started. "You absolutely deserve to feel joy...to have joy in your life, despite everything else going on right now. And wait, what happened with Margot?"

I should have known she was going to want to dive more into that comment—and I wasn't sure that I really wanted to. But since I told Gen anything and everything, I enlightened her—just a little bit. "So, before my hike with Pierre, I kind of confronted Margot about the contents of the letter, asked her if she knew anything about my father and Leo, why my mom lied. It didn't go very far before Pierre came and picked me up at Frangipane. It's been kind of a tough situation, with Margot being his mom and all, but it was his idea to start with her for any answers. I mean she is...was my mother's best friend. And I can't shake the way she responded when I asked about all of it," I said, trying to keep my voice low so Pierre wouldn't hear me.

Although it was his idea, I still felt awkward talking about his mother with him in the other room.

"Jesus, Jules. What in the hell is going on over there?" she asked rhetorically but curiously.

"Honestly, if I knew, I probably wouldn't have stayed," I answered matter-of-factly.

"Just be careful. Remember, curiosity killed the cat," she said, which for some reason sent a shiver up my spine. "Oh hey, Doll. My lunch break is about to be over, but again, just be careful and fill me in with anything you find out. Also, enjoy that lovely Frenchman with no guilt, got it? I love you, and oh, I expect you to send me that photo of him ASAP."

I laughed. "Okay, got it. I love you, too, Gen."

After I hung up the phone with Gen, I quickly sent her the photo I had just taken of Pierre sleeping. I grabbed my journal while I drank my coffee and waited for Pierre to wake up. Five seconds later, I received a text back from Gen replying to the photo of Pierre:

HOT DAMN...*drool face emoji*

Letting out a small laugh, I sat back down at the island and put the pen to paper, letting my feelings flow freely onto the page. I was falling for Pierre, and he gave me all the writing inspiration I needed.

I just felt guilty for being happy at all. I've heard that people can have a way of helping you through loss and grief, through the healing process if you let them. That was Pierre to me—he was the vessel that was healing me from the loss and betrayal I felt toward my mother. I guess in a way he was bringing out the best in me, helping me uncover more of myself the more time we spent together. Helping me want to forgive without the intention of doing so.

"Good morning, darling," I heard Pierre say as he was making his way down the stairs into the kitchen.

I shut my journal as I felt his warm hands on my shoulders. Kissing the top of my head I returned his "good morning" and placed my hand over his.

He gave my shoulders a squeeze before making his way to the coffee drip. "What are you working on, love?" he asked as he poured himself a cup.

"Oh, just making some notes in my journal." I smiled coyly, shutting the journal. "I've had quite the inspiration lately."

I could feel his smile, even though his back was turned to me. "Is that so?"

He turned to face me. "It is so," I said, grinning. "How did you sleep?"

He winked, taking a sip of his coffee while holding his gaze on me. "Probably the best I have in a long time."

"Hmm, likewise," I said, placing my elbow on the island and pressing my cheek to my fist.

Pierre left shortly after so he could get ready for his work week. Having spent the weekend with him was nothing short of magical and much needed. For the time being, I decided to let Margot stew over my questions just a little longer.

Today, I would get dressed and explore Paris on my own a little. I actually found enjoyment in doing things on my own, because everything was on my own time; I had nowhere specific to be, didn't have to answer to anyone's wants or needs. I just got to be myself and do all the things I wanted to. I really needed that right now.

I called Bernard to see if he could pick me up in thirty minutes, and he gladly obliged.

I went outside to wait for him after twenty-five minutes and looked down at my phone to see a text from Pierre:

Miss you already, beautiful. The sweetness and charm continued in overwhelming amounts.

I texted back:

Feeling the same way. I hope you have a wonderful work week :)

I put my phone in my bag when I saw Bernard pull up in his black town car.

I stepped inside the passenger side and greeted him. "Bonjour, Bernard."

"Bonjour, mademoiselle Jules. Where to today?" he asked properly.

"You know, I'm not sure. Just wanting to explore Paris for a few hours, clear my head. Any recommendations?" I asked.

"Absolutely, mademoiselle," he began. "For starters, have you had petit-déjeuner, yet?" he asked, his mustache turning up into a cheesy smile.

The mention of breakfast made my stomach grumble. "As a matter of fact, I haven't. And the hunger bug just hit. Anywhere you recommend besides Frangipane and Pain d'Amour?" I asked, wanting to avoid Margot but also wanting to try the other amazing cafés Paris had to offer.

"Where to even start...there are plenty!" Bernard pointed out enthusiastically before continuing, "However, if I had to pick my highest recommendation, it would have to be Café du Soleil. They have sélections savoureuses...tasty."

"Cafe of the Sun? Sounds plenty tasty to me. Will you please drop me off there to start?" I requested per his recommendation.

"Certainly." He smiled before driving off onto the cobblestone road.

I took note of the fall foliage almost taking complete hold—where the leaves were once green turning into gold, they were now gold turning into burnt orange and red. The colors lent themselves well to the brilliant architecture that surrounds the city. Fall was coming into full force, signifying that time continued on with or without you, and it hit me like a ton of bricks as I stared out the window of the car: nothing stayed stagnant.

Bernard was right. Café du Soleil was amazing. I had what the locals call a "traditional French breakfast": a fresh-baked croissant with butter and jam and a cup of freshly brewed espresso (with a teaspoon of brown sugar for my liking).

After breakfast, I had Bernard drive me to one of the renowned tiny villages nestled in Paris: Montmartre.

With its cobbled streets, stunning Sacré-Cœur basilica, and art culture, Montmartre was no doubt full of charm. It's perched on the top of a small hill in the 18th arrondissement, the most famous Parisian district that has lost none of its village atmosphere, which has appealed to many artists of the 19th and 20th centuries. Bernard said it's a real melting pot of art and inspiration for the cinema.

Bernard dropped me off on the main street of the village, so I could walk around and do my own exploring.

"What time would you like me to pick you up back here, mademoiselle?" he asked before I stepped out of the town car.

"Does three work? That should give me plenty of time to explore, right?"

"Most certainly, mademoiselle. I'll meet you back here at precisely three," he confirmed, smiling.

"Merci, Bernard," I said as I stepped out of the car onto the cobbled street. With my left hand lingering on the top of the door before I closed it, I turned around, placing my right hand on the top of the door, peeking my head inside. "By the way, Bernard, please call me Jules." I wasn't sure why I hadn't corrected him before but better late than never.

"Very well, mademoi...Jules." he nodded.

Smiling, I stood up straight and closed the car door.

After a couple of hours of wandering the village and a delicious lunch at the cutest café, I stumbled upon a little book shop. It had an adorable pink storefront with pastel green shutters and the same bed of flowers that seemed to adorn every window in

Paris. I stepped through the pastel green Dutch door into the shop that had three walls of floor-to-ceiling bookcases, each with retractable rolling library ladders like in Beauty and the Beast.

I shut the door behind me after my eyes roamed the shop for a few seconds, taking in how cute and rustic it was.

The person working was busy with another customer, so I took it upon myself to meander around the store. I ran my fingers along the book spines lined on the left side of the store bookshelves and thought of Pierre.

There is something beautiful and respectful about art in general, but especially art in the form of writing. For as long as we can remember, writing has been a tool to communicate for humans, a way of expressing your thoughts. Writing can serve to transform the intangibility of a person's emotions and experiences into something more.

Through my thoughts I came to the realization of why Pierre was so passionate about being an acquisition editor. He got to read the raw, unedited versions of a person's emotions and experiences in a tangible way.

"Puis-je vous aider à manquer?" A male voice with a French accent sounded from behind me, severing my thoughts.

Turning around I replied, "Ah je ne parle pas français," explaining I didn't understand what he said, because I don't speak French. I made sure to master this phrase.

"Ahh, excuse-moi, I mean, excuse me, miss," he corrected himself. "How may I help you?"

"No worries, merci." I knew "thank you" at least. "Do you have any historical fiction books you recommend?" I asked, remembering Pierre said that was one of the genres Hachette Livre publishes.

"Absolutely. Right this way," he said, leading me to the bookshelves that lined the back wall of the store. "I recommend *The Women of Chateau Burgundy* by Dreyfus Meyers," he said, pulling the book off the shelf and handing it to me. I flipped it over to skim the back as he explained what it was about. "It's about a castle in France and the women bound to it by its legacy. How the duty to your country is above all, and the hope, love and courage, resilience and perseverance, and the strength and burdens we take from those of our lineages."

"Sounds intriguing," I said, opening the book to the copyrights page. I moved my finger down the page to see Hachette Livre indeed published this book. "I'll take it," I said, smiling at the man who helped me.

"Excellent," he said. "Is there anything else I can help you with, miss?"

"I think this will do it. I appreciate it," I thanked him.

Waving his hand toward the checkout counter, he said, "You are most certainly welcome. Right this way."

Everyone was so polite here, contrary to things I've heard about French people being rude. Maybe I just haven't encountered those people, yet, thankfully. Although, I thought back to how rude I thought Pierre was at first and huffed to myself.

The man told me my total, I paid, and then walked out of the store. I looked at my watch and saw that it was almost three, so I headed back to where Bernard dropped me off.

As I walked back, blending in with the sea of locals and other tourists, it dawned on me that I really needed this time to myself. It didn't require me to feel intense grief and betrayal. Time to myself also meant waffling back and forth in my mind on if I should take Pierre's advice and continue looking for answers, or just hold onto my peace of mind and take Gen's advice of keeping my curiosity at bay on this topic. My gut feeling was right in the middle, which was of no use to me.

There aren't many things that are cut and dry, black and white. And this was one of the many that wasn't.

twenty

On the car ride back to the chalet, it hit me.

Why hadn't I asked Bernard more about my mother? Surely, being her driver, there may have been things he picked up on, like places she went, people she was with.

So with that logic, I broke the silence.

"Hey, Bernard. I have a question for you," I said as we glided across the familiar cobblestone.

"Oui, Jules?" he replied, never taking his eyes off the road, or his hands off the wheel.

"How well did you know my mother?" I asked bluntly.

"Hmm, we had a lot of, how you say it, small talk. She remained private for the most part. Why do you ask?" I trusted my instincts and chose to believe Bernard was telling the truth.

"No reason in particular just wanting to know what her life was like here, is all." I half-lied. Not being completely satisfied with his answer, I pressed a little harder. "Did she ever ride around with anyone?"

"As a matter of fact, yes." Now we were getting somewhere. "Monsieur Leo. When Madame Esmée got sick, he was with her often, to and from doctor's appointments. He never left her out of his sight, it appeared. He took good care of your mother," he said, making me instantly feel horrible for not being there for my mother, while a perfect stranger was. I couldn't have been, because I didn't know she was sick, but why was I questioning Leo?

"Thank you, Bernard," I said, staring out the window, feeling more and more like I should just drop the entire *investigation* and accept the facts despite Pierre's suggestion.

"Certainly, Jules," he said, pulling up to the chalet to drop me off.

What a day.

I thanked Bernard for dropping me off and walked up the cobblestone path leading to the cottage. Walking through the door and kicking off my shoes, it didn't take much time for me to pour myself a glass of red wine. I pulled the book out of my bag, and with my glass of wine, took a seat in the oversized chair in front of the fireplace. I texted Pierre to pick his brain about it, then shortly after, I drifted off.

Have any plans for lunch? Pierre texted me on Wednesday. He had texted me here and there over the last few days but had been bogged down with manuscripts, so I gave him his space to work, as I understood better than anyone else the meaning of strict deadlines.

I had just woken up and made my drip coffee, pleasantly surprised to hear from him—on a weekday in the middle of a work day nonetheless.

As a matter of fact, my day is wide open, I replied.

Merveilleuse. Interested in meeting me at Canal Saint-Martin? I have a surprise for you, he said. A surprise? I wasn't a fan of surprises, but I was genuinely excited to see what he had planned.

Absolutely. What time? I asked.

Does noon on the dot work? he asked.

See you then :) I replied.

See you then :) he repeated.

I put on a pair of jeans, high-neck tank, and Oxford loafers, hoping I wasn't over or underdressed for whatever Pierre had planned.

Bernard drove me to Canal Saint-Martin by the pedestrian overpass that went over the canal. The trees were shades of gold, speckles of them brushing the sidewalk that lined the water. It was absolutely beautiful here.

I spotted Pierre where he said he would be. He reminded me of a dashing Chris Hemsworth as I approached him. When he saw me walking up, he smiled in adoration.

"Hi, beautiful," he uttered, pressing his lips to mine and pulling me in for a gentle yet secure hug.

"Hi, handsome." I smiled after he let go. "So, what are we doing here?" I asked with twinkling eyes that only looked at him this way.

"Right this way," he said, holding out his hand. The way in which he was mysterious captivated me, causing excitement to grow with every moment I was with him.

There was a cobblestone path on either side of the narrow canal parallel to ledges that overlooked the water, people lining it as far as I could see. Pierre led me to a spot on the path under a tree that had a picnic blanket and basket set up.

"After you," he said, waving his hand toward the blanket.

"Pierre...you did this for me?" I asked rhetorically, flattered and admiring the gesture unlike anything anyone has ever done for me.

"Oui." He smiled as I lowered down onto the blanket. He followed suit, so we were sitting side-by-side.

"This is amazing. Thank you so much, really," I expressed.

"It was no trouble at all," he said, opening up the picnic basket and taking out two plastic cups and a bottle of champagne. He poured the champagne into the cups and handed me one. "Cheers," he said, raising his cup, and I clinked mine with his.

"Cheers," I said, taking a sip. "So, how did you manage to slip away from work?"

He laughed the sweetest sound I had ever heard. "That's a good question. Let's just say, I moved a few things around on my schedule." He winked.

Satisfied with that answer, I intended to soak up every minute of him making time for me.

We spent about an hour talking and laughing, eating sandwiches and fruit, feeding each other strawberries here and there, and finishing the bottle of champagne.

Pierre was everything I had ever wanted in a man—tall, handsome, passionate, attentive, fun, thoughtful. I was falling for him in each moment he offered to me, and I only hoped he was feeling the same way.

october

twenty-one

Pierre and I were spending a lot of time together. Days somehow turned into weeks, but with Pierre it felt like time was standing still, like we were in our own little time zone. Luckily Paris' beautiful fall foliage reminded us that time was indeed passing, as each day the leaves slowly turned varying colors of gold and auburn. Fall was in full force, and the piles of colorful foliage were forming on the ground. The air was getting more brisk but refreshing.

It was October now, and I realized falling in love with Pierre was inevitable—at the same time, I felt like I had so many unanswered questions about my mother...and my father...and had gotten nowhere with trying to figure out why I had even decided to stay in Paris. Maybe it was all a part of a bigger scheme. One I chose not to see at the moment.

Don't get me wrong, Pierre was enough of a reason—but I still couldn't shake the feeling something felt wrong, still. Maybe my instincts had been clouded by grief, leading me astray this time. Maybe I was going down a downward spiral, pulling something out of nothing. I was in the same skin that I came here in. I wore the same clothes I did in Boston, used the same shampoo, and still enjoyed the same wine. Yet, I still felt like a stranger to myself, shaking hands with a woman I didn't yet know. I didn't have a choice. This new version of me was happening whether I was ready for it or not. This is what grief did to me.

Pierre came over, and we were lying on the couch, with the fireplace lit, watching a movie and drinking wine. I was lying next to him, my right leg draped over his, and my right arm over his torso, head resting on his chest.

"So have you talked to my mother lately?" he asked me.

"Nope. Not since the day we went on that hike." I responded skeptically. My conversation with Margot was left open-ended, causing a swirl of uneasiness that formed within me. "Have you?"

"No, I guess I haven't. I've been working and spending any free time I have with you honestly." *We should start with my mother*, Pierre's words echoed in my mind. Not wanting to press when either of us would talk to Margot, I changed the subject.

I had been in Paris for two months, and I was starting to realize my purpose for being here had changed—I had changed, my heart had changed. I came here so angry with my mother for not telling me she was sick, and then when I got here, I was even more angry with her for lying about my father. But as each day passed by, no step closer to any semblance of truth about my father, I felt myself wanting to let go of the past.

One Sunday afternoon, the first day that was actually cool enough that you needed a jacket, Pierre and I decided to take a walk at the park.

Walking hand in hand, he casually asked me a question I had always tried to avoid at all costs, because the ideas scared me. "What do you think about marriage and kids?"

"Hmm, that's kind of random..." I trailed off, not sure of how to answer this question.

"Well, I feel like we have talked a lot about our parents, our careers, but not much about our futures, and what we want out of life, other than work."

He had a point.

I guess the truth was, I didn't think about having this type of conversation with Pierre, because I was going back to Boston next month. I didn't exactly know what that meant for us, but I also knew that what I felt for him wasn't just a fling.

So, I entertained his question and answered him honestly, "Well...I've never had an example of what a good marriage even looks like. But despite all I've been through, I still believe in love, and I still have hope I'll find the person who will change my views on what a good marriage looks like. The kind you probably only read about, but I'm sure it exists...somewhere," I said. Before he could respond I moved on to the second part of his question. "I haven't really thought about kids much." I studied his profile, trying to gauge his reaction. "But again, I'm sure the right person will come along, the one I will want to marry and have babies with...one day."

I felt like my expression and feelings were fairly neutral at this explanation. I wasn't sure if Pierre would be this guy for me, but I kind of hoped maybe he would be.

"I appreciate your honesty. I personally want a wife and a beautiful baby girl who looks just like her, and I want to give them both the world, not take it from them. And Jules, for what it's worth, when I look at you, I see someone who despite having been hurt and disappointed so many times by everyone they have ever loved, you still not only believe in love but you know *how* to love." He stopped walking and turned to face me, taking both of my hands in his before he cupped my face with them. Staring into my eyes, he confessed, "And that is one of many reasons I'm falling for you. You are a beautiful person. I mean that."

Closing my eyes, I pressed my lips to his for a few beats, and he pulled me closer into his body.

Once our kiss broke, I said, "Thank you for seeing me."

I realized at that moment that Pierre wanted to show me the world, his world, and more than anything, I wanted to let him. I wanted to explore everything that made him happy: people, places, things. I wake up every morning, and the first thing I want to do is see his face, and the human behind the face who washes away all the pain and sadness I have felt, have been feeling in my life. You would think being abandoned by my father and betrayed by my mother—the two people whose love and trust I needed the most–would have broken me or made me run away from any chance at real love, but it didn't, at least not with him.

I was starting to believe we had a consummate love—the kind we are all ultimately hoping for—the combination of intimacy, passion and commitment that is unmatched. The kind of love you think of when you find your soulmate—the all-consuming love. The kind that makes you embrace how much pain you have felt, but makes it better, because their love is like a warm blanket around you all the time. It comforts you when you need it most and never fails to make you feel beautiful, no matter how broken you are. This is how Pierre made me feel in such a small amount of time, and it was nothing short of admirable love. I didn't know how this was possible nor did I know how it even made sense, but to each other, somehow we just made sense. And that was enough.

After we got back to the chalet, we made love.

It had felt different this time—like admitting to each other how we felt strengthened our physical bond.

As we laid in bed, my head on his chest, I pressed my ear deeper into it. I committed his heartbeat to memory, feeling like both of ours were beating at the same pace, the same rhythm, in sync, at this moment, for the same purpose—to love each other.

With the way he looked at me and saw me, with his touch, and with his words I knew he uttered only for me, it sent shivers down every fiber of my being.

twenty-two

When I met Pierre at the Pont des Arts bridge—where we had first met—it was the first snowfall of the season. Soft, white powder lined the ground, the tops of the buildings, and the bridge railing—the one Pierre was leaning up against as I walked toward him.

The snow continued to flurry down lightly, so there weren't many people out and about, and it was like the moment, the bridge, was just for him and me to take up space in. I took my time walking up to him, so I could soak in every inch of the way he was staring at me—each time was like he was looking at me for the first time, *seeing* me for the first time.

He ran a hand through his disheveled hair, beaming a smile he reserved for me. He was wearing a long, gray trench coat that of course accentuated his gray eyes and under the flurry, they looked more charcoal.

This was the simple moment I realized I had undoubtedly fallen in love with him—that feeling was amazing, and terrifying, at the same time, because I knew my time in Paris was coming to an end, but I could see him so clearly, like I was walking toward what could be my future.

When I was to leave in a few weeks, I didn't have a clue where that would leave us. I was going back to Boston, and Pierre was staying in Paris, and all I knew was I couldn't have a relationship with someone who was 3,400 miles away. *Should I ask him to go with me?* was the question I had been constantly asking myself.

But for now, I was going to embrace all this love he had to offer while I could—and just pretend the inevitable conversation of us going our separate ways wasn't going to happen. *Would he say yes?* I wondered.

The last few steps I lightly jogged to him and jumped in his arms, as he picked me up off the ground, I curled my hands around the back of his neck, threading my fingers through his thick hair. I pulled him toward me and planted my lips on his. This kiss was different from all the others—it was more passionate, more desperate, making my heart thump harder and faster with every movement; this kiss confirmed the way he was feeling was the way I was. He set me down, and we searched each other's eyes for a moment, like they were doing the talking for us.

"You look absolutely beautiful as always," he said, breaking the silence, his dimples prominent in the way I loved.

Although the weather was turning colder, I felt like I was regaining the color in my life that had been lost when I found out my mother died. Pierre was to blame for that.

"Thank you." I smiled in admiration, putting my hands to my cheeks, which had warmed up from the heat crawling up my neck.

"Let's walk," he said, reaching for my hand, planting a light kiss on it before walking us on the bridge, to the exact spot we ran into each other for the first time.

We paused at the spot—our spot—our gazes fixated on the glassy blue Seine River. I heard light ripples in the water from birds flying by, and we embraced the comfortable silence that came with being in each other's presence, before Pierre said the words that changed our discourse.

He turned to face me, grabbing my hands between his clammy and warm ones, despite the cold. "Jules...I need to tell you something."

My heart dropped, knowing all too well not many conversations starting with those words could be a good thing.

As a million things ran through my head, one thing came to mind that I was hoping he would tell me at this moment—one of the good things.

I love you.

If these were the words that were coming, I may have debated staying in Paris myself versus asking him to come with me. My world would have changed by these three little but big words.

But, as fate would have it, those weren't the words to slip from his beautiful mouth—right now, anyway. However, his words would still change my world.

"We kind of met by accident but partially didn't..." he started, leaving me confused. His eyebrows were creased, but I couldn't see his eyes. He was still staring at my hands while shifting on his feet nervously causing my heart to race.

My expression fell, and the lighthearted tone I usually had when we talked quickly dissipated. "What do you mean? Sure we did. I mean, we are standing in the very spot we met...right here."

I backed away from him, holding my hands out to my sides open.

"I know we met right *here*, but what I'm saying is I knew you would be here. Although I didn't know it was *you*, I knew you would be here," he tried to explain, but the revelation still wasn't making any sense to me.

The words fell from his mouth, and I felt like I was at a standstill, like the world had literally stopped trying to decipher what the hell he was talking about.

"I...I don't understand, Pierre..." I trailed off, fully perplexed. I squinted, breathing heavier as I tried to piece together what he was saying, my heart racing faster and faster, like its beating was trying to keep up with my breathing.

"That's what I'm trying to explain. My mother said you would be here. I thought it was a long shot finding you on this bridge, but there you were looking so sad but so beautiful," he explained, his body stone cold now. It took everything in me to let him continue, but at the same time, my body was numb with every word. I couldn't move, and I couldn't talk, even if I wanted to. "It was on short notice, so I didn't even get the photo she sent of you until after we had met. She asked if I could keep you company while you were here...to help ease your mind and pain. It wasn't anything vindictive, but I really didn't expect to fall in love, either," he clarified, as I was recalling Margot recommending I come here after telling her I would be staying in Paris a little longer. "Long story short, we did meet by *accident*, but I knew to come here looking for someone with your description...looking for *you*."

Discontent laced my features as my heart fell from my chest. I couldn't believe he kept this from me the whole time. Anger was brewing inside of me faster than my mother's espresso machine brewed coffee. The only sound I could hear now was the fast breaths releasing through my nostrils as I panted. I let him continue as I stood before him bewildered.

"Jules, I couldn't stand it if I hurt you. Tell me what you're thinking," he said, taking a step closer as I took a step back. His shoulders dropped as he sighed, panicking as he started talking faster. "I didn't tell you, because I didn't think it was relevant. Although my mother technically set us up, every word, every feeling has been absolutely real. And I did fall in love with you."

There they were—the words I wanted to hear—but not in this way, not following the words of betrayal, the words that made me question everything we were.

"I...I can't believe this. Why would Margot do that...why would you do that?" I stuttered, shaking my head in disbelief, trying to make sense of their actions.

My veins were filled with shock. The words *I love you* were so big, yet so small in light of his confession. Could they really mean anything when this was a pity love setup by his mother, following my mother's death? They were a lie, just like everything and everyone else in my life. There were so many lies. Lies of death, lies of love, lies of fathers and secret lives. In the end, it seemed Gen was the only person I could trust, and I thought that was Pierre, too—until now.

"No one wanted to hurt you, amour—" he started before I interrupted him.

I held up a hand so he'd quit adding to the pile of lies. "Stop with the charming *my loves* and the *my darlings*, Pierre. Cut the shit. This whole time our relationship has been a...lie? The last thing I expected when I came here for my mother's memorial service was to find love, too. And I did, with you. And to now find out it was all a setup, do you know how hurtful that is? I feel like you just ripped my damn heart from my chest. What am I going to find out next? Please tell me you haven't been keeping anything else from me," I pleaded through strained breaths. I couldn't possibly take anymore, all the while, I *needed* to know everything.

My heart was hammering inside of me as I paced back and forth, feeling my feet slip on the dusting of snow. But I couldn't stop. I kept moving, because once I stopped, I'd crumble beneath my feet.

His beautiful features turned ice cold, as I braced myself for the words to escape from his mouth next. "There is something else, but to be honest, I didn't think it was my place to tell you. And it's something I found out only a few days ago, Jules—"

Stabbing him in the eyes with my icy glare, I demanded through gritted teeth, "What the fuck is going on, Pierre?" I glared at him, my eyes begging him to just spit out the worst of it all, if that's where this was leading to.

He took a full breath of crisp, frigid air then exhaled before shaking my entire world with the truth I had waited twenty-seven years to hear—the truth I had yearned for my mother to utter, the truth she danced around in her letter and for my entire life that I was just starting to let go of.

Putting his hands in his coat pockets, he rocked back and forth. "It's about your father..." he trailed off in what felt like slow motion.

"What about him?!" I begged and shouted.

"Leo and your mother." My vision was blurry with tears as I had an inkling where this was headed now. "Jules, Leo...he's your father. That's why he was here for her when she got sick."

My heart was pounding as I held my hands over my mouth, speechless and in disbelief at what Pierre had just told me. I felt like I was in another nightmare, only this time, I didn't wake up.

My hands dropped from my face as I struggled for words. "I can't...I can't...oh my god. Is this really true?"

I knew the answer, but I needed to hear it again in case I was dreaming. Was this another one of my nightmares? It was, but this time, I was awake. The tears fell freely the more helpless I felt.

You would think that him telling me the truth about my father trumped any anger I had felt over how we met. But I was feeling so many emotions right now that I didn't even know I had, and I was completely shredded inside by the way this truth had been released into the cold, open air. He may have had the decency to tell me the truth when no one else did, not even my own mother, but I was still furious. *Has my time here all been a mistake?*

My body was trembling before he pleaded, "Jules, come here." With hesitation, I let him wrap my lifeless frame into his arms, which he held tightly around me, as I sobbed into his shoulder.

"I'm here for you in any way you need me to be. I meant what I said...I love you," he reiterated. "I'm not going anywhere. I'm not your dad. I'm not Leo."

Those words *your dad* now held a new meaning. I now know who he really is, and I could have known him this whole time I was in Paris had I known. But Pierre told me Leo knew but so did Margot. He had found the answer to the question I had been longing for, the original purpose for me staying in Paris. *Should I have tried harder to find them myself? Was it Margot's plan all along to keep me distracted from finding out the truth?* The same answer I tried only once to get from Margot as she lied to my face. The answer Pierre told me I should not stop looking for, but I did, because I was so wrapped up in him. I felt like Margot had spit on my grave, along with Leo. More like they danced on it together holding hands.

I felt betrayal in so many ways, and when Pierre uttered those three words again, I wanted so much to prove love would overshadow any moment of darkness. As I knew I had an entirely new challenge ahead of me, the only words I could manage were, "I don't believe you. Now if you'll excuse me, I need to go do something."

I knew better than anyone that you can't live long with your head in the clouds. What goes up must come down.

twenty-three

I rushed back to the chalet and pulled out the letter my mother wrote that I had stuck in a drawer. I reread it again and again, analyzing it with a fine-toothed comb. There was no mention of Leo. *Why was it so cryptic?* Out of all the lies, the least my mother could have done was write a straightforward letter that didn't leave me insane.

Scratching my head and rubbing my forehead, trying not to pull my hair out from frustration, I got nothing new from it. The fury grew within me, and I angrily crumpled the piece of paper up into a ball and threw it on the floor. The sound of the thin piece of paper hitting the hardwood floor made me more displeased.

Tipping my head back, staring at the white ceiling, I took a deep breath. When I straightened back up, my gaze hit the crinkled letter again.

It was only then that I noticed something was scribbled on the back of it in really small handwriting I hadn't noticed when I read it the first few times. I immediately jumped to my feet to pick the paper up off the ground and hurriedly unfolded it out of its ball with shaking hands. After I had straightened it out, I laid it on the desk and tried to smooth it out as much as possible so it would be legible. There was one tiny word on the back: *Leo*. Was that her way of telling me Leo is my father? This was fifty shades of fucked up, and I wanted to crawl into a ball and die.

I crumpled the piece of paper back into a ball and sobbed uncontrollably into my closed fists. "Why, MOM! Why did you do this to me?" I asked a ghost.

I clutched my chest, gasping for any ounce of air I could get. The pain in my chest grew as I rubbed it with my hand. I allowed the sobs to subside before making a call to someone I didn't want to get into it with but had the information I needed at this moment—Margot. I had my own bone to pick with her at a later time.

After a few rings and the feeling I was going to get her voicemail, she picked up. "Hey, Jules, listen I—"

Surely Pierre had already told her he told me about Leo.

"Margot, I really don't want to talk about that right now with you," I cut her off. "I only called, so I could get *his* number."

Without hesitation, she answered, "Yes, of course." Knowing exactly who I meant confirmed Pierre did tell her that he told me about Leo.

After she gave me the number and we hung up, I made the phone call that changed my life.

I called Leo, who was surprised to hear from me. I guess no one gave him the heads up I would be calling like Margot gave Pierre, or he was acting surprised to hear from me. "Hello?" He answered the phone.

Trying to keep my voice from shaking, so I could play it cool, I said, "Hey, Leo...it's Juliette."

"Juliette?"

"Yea..." I trailed off. "I have some, uh, questions...about my mother. Would you be able to meet me, like now?" I tried not to sound too demanding, but I was desperate to stitch up this lie once and for all.

He agreed to meet me downtown at Café L'Orange. I questioned myself if meeting in a public space was a good idea or not right now. I wasn't thinking clearly, however, and I would have taken him up on any offer to meet anywhere. I needed an olive branch at this moment.

The car ride over to the café was all a blur. I was sure Bernard was trying to talk to me, but I was so worked up I couldn't formulate any responses. I kept biting my fingernails, and my gaze was fixed on looking through the car window, but my brain wasn't accepting any images.

When Bernard had dropped me off in front of the café, Leo was out front sitting at a little bistro table. I paused on the sidewalk as I took note of the way he looked, my heart pounding out of my chest. His disheveled wavy brown hair had subtle streaks of gray in them, along with his stubble, even more so than when I had last seen him to spread my mother's ashes. He appeared worn down, with prominent wrinkles that had formed around his eyes. How so much had changed between then and now.

He looked up at me with tired blue eyes and furrowed brows, pursing his lips into a straight line, just shy of a smile. *Had he known why I called, why I needed to meet him urgently? Had the truth been eating away at him?*

It was at this moment, us locking eyes for a single moment, I thought back to the faint and vague memories I had of my father. They were difficult to recall, all muffled, but I remember *his dark hair, those crystal blue eyes, the stubble on his face that lightly brushed across mine like sandpaper when he held me, the way he smelled of musk and sandalwood.* It was the same man before me now—just twenty-seven years older.

I took a deep breath, steeling myself, and still unsure of what I was going to say to him. *What could I say?* As I slowly walked toward the bistro table, I couldn't think of anything I could say to bring back the twenty-seven years I had lost, that he had *missed*.

He stood up to greet me, reaching out his shaky hand toward me. "Hello, Jules," he said with a quivering voice.

"It's *Juliette*," I corrected him sternly. I felt like I had no control over what was to come next.

He nodded then waved his hand toward the empty seat across from him. "My apologies. Please, have a seat."

I wasn't sure if I wanted to take a seat across from the man who had abandoned me all these years. Standing like a statue stuck in its place, I was reluctant to continue with this meeting, with this conversation. My fight-or-flight mode kicked into full gear, and I wanted to just run away now, to avoid facing this man who had a choice to stay, but he made the choice to leave. *Should I just make the choice to leave now?*

"Juliette?" he uttered, bringing me back to the current moment.

"Huh?" It took a moment to step out of my mind, while I made a decision.

"Want to sit?" he reiterated, giving me another opportunity to flee. But, I was tired of running. I came here with a purpose, and I needed to see it through.

Nodding, we both sat down simultaneously, our eyes never leaving one another. I glared at him, but all I saw was a coward—not a father, not *my* father.

A waitress stopped by our table and said, "Bonjour, mademoiselle. May I—"

I held up my hand, cutting her off and said, "We are good for now, merci."

She shot me a dirty look and a tight-lipped smile before nodding and walking away, leaving Leo and me in the dark abyss that was this confrontation.

My gut was wrenched at this moment, and my heart was racing faster, as if it couldn't be beating too fast already, like it wanted to reach the finish line, the finale of this movie. I had waited twenty-seven years to face the man sitting across from me again—to know him. What hurt the most was that my mother reconnected with him at some point—when she had returned to Paris following my high school graduation—and she had every opportunity to tell me, and so did he, but they chose not to. I felt like I would never know her intentions behind her actions—all I had to go off of was a fucking letter, and even through that it felt like she sent me on a pointless—and painful—scavenger hunt.

"You know why I asked you to meet me, don't you?" I asked him, staring at him blankly, as he stared down at the table, toying with the stem of his coffee mug he'd ordered before I arrived.

"I think I have an idea," he said, our gazes now fixated on each other, ignoring the buzz on the street around us. "Who told you?"

The sounds of the running cars and chatter from people were drowned out by my mission. "Does that matter?" I asked, raising my tone above the others in the restaurant, a few glances shooting my way. "Is it true or not, Leo? Cut the *shit*. Are you my father?" My voice started to tremble, and tears welled in my eyes, causing the vision of him to blur, much like how I felt about him.

Twenty-seven years. The last twenty-seven missed birthdays, having my heart broken for the first time, learning how to drive, graduating from high school, from college, landing my dream job, losing my *mother*. He wasn't there for any of it, and not because he fell off the face of the earth, but because he *chose* not to. The words of my mother's letter were bleeding into my brain: *she didn't want me growing up knowing he didn't want me.* Now I was determined to find out why.

He said with a broken voice, "Yes, it's true." Pain laced his tone while he pinched his eyebrows together and the bridge of his nose, looking down again, as if feeling defeated and trying to hold in tears.

But I couldn't hold in mine. A tear slipped down my cheek, and I quickly wiped it away, not wanting him to see how weak he had made me. "Look at me," I demanded. When it took him a few seconds, I said again just below a shout, "Fucking look at me!" All manners escaped me, and my words and harsh tone caused a few bystanders to look our way again, and he obliged. "Just tell me *why*. How could you leave me at three years old, face me at my mother's fucking memorial, and at the spreading of her ashes, and not say anything. Do you not have a fucking heart?" The words came out like vomit, and that's exactly what I felt like doing as they came out.

"Juliette, it's a lot more *complicated* than that. You have to believe—"

I interrupted him, "How could I *ever* believe a goddamn word you say?" Or anyone else for that matter.

I was furious, I was sad, I was hurt, I was disappointed. I felt like I was in middle school, wondering what I had done so wrong to deserve this—from him, from my mother, from Margot. They had all taken a knife and killed me with a thousand cuts over the last twenty-seven years.

"I'm begging you, please hear me out," he pleaded, narrowing his eyes, his lips trembling. He looked like he had aged another five years just sitting here with me.

I nodded and let out a huff, and I wasn't sure I could hear another word from the man who had abandoned me. But I let him continue, desperate to know the truth.

"When I found out your mother was pregnant, she had told me you weren't mine. I had been back and forth between Boston and Paris on business, and she told me she had slept with someone else. I even stayed, until you were three, because I loved her, I loved *you,* as if you were my own, and I wanted to make the situation work. But then she broke things off and decided she wanted to raise you on her own. I had no *choice.*"

His words were making no sense to me. My heart dropped, but at the same time the rest of my body felt numb again. Why would my mother lie and make me grow up without a father? Did he really not have a choice?

I knitted my eyebrows together. "I don't understand...how did you end up back in her life then?"

"I didn't find out you were really mine until Esmée was diagnosed with cancer. She had called me and told me she needed help. I hadn't heard from her for nearly twenty-seven years. But this was the woman I believed to be the true love of my life, and she was dying. I couldn't bring myself to let her be alone during this time, no matter how much pain she had caused me in the past. She finally came clean about the whole thing and told me her parents forced her to end things with me because I'm American, and they wanted her to move back to Paris, or she would be cut off—financially and from the family. Apparently she ended up staying in Boston, because she didn't want to move you around, but by then, the damage had already been done. When I saw you again at your mother's service, I saw so much of her in you. The way you look like her, spoke like her, and I felt like I was looking at your mother twenty-seven years ago. I just didn't know how to tell you, Juliette, and I didn't think it was an appropriate time, either. I didn't want to disrupt your life any further than it already has been.

I ended up staying here after she passed, because I have some clients, and I didn't know how to leave yet."

My mouth was wide open the entire time he spoke the truth about why my mother lied. After all this time, it came down to my grandparents who ended up passing away two years after she moved back when I went to college. The whole web of lies seemed so silly in the grand scheme of things, yet destroyed multiple lives in the process. I didn't even know what Leo did for work, or what he loved to do on the weekends, if he ever got married, if he had any other children.

I only knew where he—still—lived. My voice had dropped down to nearly a whisper. "You still live in Boston?" All he could manage was a wordless nod while keeping his head down. "I-I really can't believe all this. It's too much," I confessed, now too stunned to shed any more tears. "Now what? Do we go about living our normal lives when we get back to Boston? Pretend none of this ever happened?"

"Well, I think that part is up to you," he admitted, searching my face for answers, as if we could just pick up from here and act like nothing happened.

When I came to Paris, I didn't know what I was going to find. I had just a few weeks left here, and now I would be leaving knowing the truth about my father and having fallen in love with a French man who lived here, while I lived in Boston.

I was now faced with not one but two dilemmas. And the truth was, I didn't know what I was going to do about either one.

twenty-four

Esmée + Leo

"*Hi, Leo, it's Esmée.*" My voice shook as I spoke into the phone.

"Esmée?" he responded, like he was talking to a ghost. I very well should have been.

"Yes, it...it's me." I wasn't sure how he would react. After all, it had been twenty-seven years since I last saw him, since we last spoke, since I crushed his soul.

"The same Esmée from—"

"Yes, twenty-seven years ago," I anxiously finished his thought.

"I see..." he trailed off. "So...with all due respect, but why are you calling me?" He didn't owe me any respect.

My hands were trembling as I held the phone, thinking I had made a mistake by calling him. What right did I have after what I had done to him? This phone call was as painful as the cancer that was invading my body. My voice continued to shake as I tried to explain my reason for calling. "Leo, I'm...I'm..." I struggled to confess that I was *dying*. It hurt to hear myself say it out loud; it became very real. "I'm dying." There was a pause on the other line, and I thought I had lost him. "Leo, you there?"

"Ye–yes, I'm here," he stammered. "Esmée, look I'm so very sorry. I don't know what to say, and I still don't know why you're calling...me."

His words cut like a knife, but he was right. Why was I calling him? After I took a moment to collect my thoughts, I remembered why. "I guess I wanted to make amends. And...make things right. I need to tell you something, and I think it would be better in person. However, I can't travel..."

"I see," he said again, but did he see? I'm sure he had no idea what was coming.

I explained to him I only had maybe two months left, and he happened to be flying to Paris the following week for a few accounts he was working on. He agreed to come to the chalet when he arrived. The truth was finally going to be released in the open air.

"How *could* you?" Leo's voice was sharp when I told him Juliette was *his*. I would die with the look on his face etched into my mind. A look of disgust, lips turned down, narrowed eyes boring into me, like I was the devil. And I was.

He stood from the couch abruptly, as if he wanted to leave right then.

"Leo, please," I pleaded with a frail voice, too weak to stand up and stop him, so I remained seated on the couch. "Please, sit. Give me a chance to explain."

"You had your chance...twenty-seven years ago."

"My parents forced me to end things with you, Leo. I didn't have a choice!"

"We all have *choices,* Esmée! And you've had to live with yours, and now die with it." His words twisted a dagger into my heart, and I clutched my chest, as if there was one really there. I sobbed uncontrollably into my hands as all the pain I have caused Leo and my daughter over the years fully sunk in. I just wanted to stop breathing right then and there. I heard him let out a big sigh and felt the couch sink beside me. He placed a hand on my back and rubbed me gently. "Esmée, I'm sorry. I shouldn't have—"

Lifting my head from my hands, I interrupted him, "No, no. You have nothing to be sorry for. You're right. I made my bed, and now I have to lie in it."

After we sat for a few moments in silence and my sobs subdued, I further explained to him why my parents wanted me to end things with him and lie about my pregnancy. They were traditional and wanted me to marry a French man and to move back to Paris. If I didn't do it their way, they were going to cut me off from the estate and cast me out. I wanted Juliette to have security for the rest of her life, to never have to worry about anything. So, when it was time to make my choice, I chose her. I didn't regret choosing her, but I did regret what the choice cost—what it cost me, Leo, and my daughter.

I don't know if Leo pitied me, because I was dying, or, I simply was the love of his life—he surely was mine—because he decided to stay and take me to appointments, to help me close things up with my estate attorney, and prepare to, well, die.

My liver started failing two weeks before I was on my deathbed—Leo by my side.

Your body is showing it's in the process of dying. It's up to you on what you want your final moments to look like, my oncologist told me. *It's time to notify your family and make you as comfortable as possible.*

I decided I wanted my final moments to be at home, not in that cold hospital room that smelled of death itself. I couldn't bring myself to tell my only daughter, my only living family that I had been in the hospital and was going home to actively *die*, to pull her away from the somewhat normal life she had built for herself, despite the brokenness I had caused in it.

I'll never forget the look on Leo's face when he told me, "I know you're dying, and it's breaking my heart, despite all we've been through…"

And that broke mine.

twenty-five

I decided to draw a warm bubble bath in the stand-alone tub. As it filled, I opened up a mini bottle of Prosecco and lit my tobacco teak candle, setting it on the bathroom counter. The candle smoke entered my nostrils, making me feel like it was in my lungs, or maybe that was just the anxiety causing clouds in my chest, suffocating me.

I linked my phone's Bluetooth to my portable speaker and contemplated how I left things with Leo after finally finding out the truth.

I think that part is up to you, his words rang in my mind.

After he had said that, I told him I needed time to think, to clear my head. There was so much to just think about I thought my head—and my heart—were going to explode.

Once the tub filled up, I carefully lowered myself into the warm, bubbly water, tipping my head back on the tub's ledge when I was submerged up to my collarbone.

The most beautiful lyrics leaked from my speaker as I closed my eyes, listening to the words as they filled my ears:

If you ever go to pieces,
Fall between the thunder clouds
I will put you back together, I won't let you down
I slip and wonder what I'd do
If you never found me, and I never found you

The lyrics gave me the epiphany that they applied to not only what my relationship could be with Leo but also with Pierre. I had some decisions to make, and neither one would be simple.

I grabbed the neck of my mini prosecco bottle, letting the crisp and smooth liquid slide down my throat. Tear droplets started to fall from my eyes, as the words of the song sank into my soul.

I wanted to have it all with Pierre, but given the circumstances, didn't know how it would work being thousands of miles apart. But what if I had never found him—or rather, what if he never found me? If I hadn't been painstakingly gripped and consumed by my mother's death, would I have ever found out Leo was my father? And now I had the opportunity to have it all with Leo—the father/daughter relationship I had longed for nearly my entire life.

I didn't know what to do nor did I want to. My life had changed here in Paris in many ways, but the way Pierre changed me, that was my favorite. He made me believe in the power of love—the kind of love that's free. However, I was faced with the fact that I would be leaving here soon, leaving him behind along with my mother's ashes, and my father in his flesh. Plus, I was still mad at him for not telling me the truth. Of the decisions to make, Pierre would be the hardest. Because I knew I was going to have to leave him, which meant dissolving the relationship that changed my life in the best way. Or, did I love him enough to ask him to go with me? How easily could I forgive him for withholding information from me, leading me on to believe one thing when the truth was another?

I grabbed my phone to see a few missed calls and texts from Pierre wondering how my meeting with Leo went. Margot must have told him I asked for Leo's number, putting two-and-two together. I deliberated ignoring his texts, maybe even leaving Paris without saying another word.

I started to text him but then I deleted it, putting my phone face down on the bathroom floor. I didn't feel like talking to anyone. I needed some time to decompress and figure things out on my own now, and that included clearing the air with Margot.

When I opened the mint green door to Frangipane, I was expecting to see Margot there. But she wasn't.

There was a younger girl working, who appeared to be college-aged. She informed me Margot was at Pain d'Amour today.

I haven't been to Margot's boulangerie yet, but Bernard knew where to take me.

I hopped back into the town car with Bernard, still having no idea what I was going to even say to her, the nerves causing me to pick at my fingers. A drive that was only ten minutes long felt like an eternity. When Bernard pulled up to the front of Pain d'Amour, my heart started pounding in my chest.

Pain d'Amour was more of an elegant chic design. The exterior was all dark wood save for the powder blue door that boasted a black and white-striped awning above it with a distressed sign that read the business name on it. A mixture of various shades of pink ranunculus flowers adorned the storefront in an arch over the door.

Taking a deep breath, I pulled the car door handle with shaking hands and stepped out of the car onto the sidewalk. People were walking by, but the sounds of the cars and chatter were drowned out by my heart pounding in my chest, ringing in my ears.

I reached for the knob of the door to the boulangerie, twisting it open slowly. Walking in, I saw Margot at the back of the shop, cashing out two customers. I waited by the door until they were walking out. Once they exited, Margot and I locked eyes as I hesitantly approached the back of the shop. The aroma of fresh baked bread filled my nose, and I tried to keep the grumbling in my stomach at bay—along with my anxiety.

She looked the same as I last saw her, but her honey brown eyes were more exhausted, the bright light that used to be in them now dim and the wrinkles around them becoming more prominent. Her lowlights were growing out, too, but every time I saw her, she still reminded me of my mother, and although the situation wasn't the best, I felt a small comfort in her presence.

"Jules..." she breathed, only my name coming out of her mouth.

"Margot."

"It's good to see you—" she started before I held up my hand to stop her.

"Please, I have to get this out." She nodded in understanding. I looked down at the floor, steeling myself, before I continued, "Twenty-seven years. Have you ever waited for something that long, Margot?"

She shook her head, pursing her lips in a straight line as tears started welling up in her eyes.

"That's how long I've waited to know the truth about my father, and you and my mom, stole that time from me."

"Jules—"

"I'm not finished," I said, interrupting her. "How long have you known?"

She was silent for about three breaths before finally answering my question. "As long as Leo has. I promise, Jules. I only found out when your mother got sick, too. This wasn't my secret to tell, and this secret, your mother truly kept to herself all these years. The only other people who knew took it to their graves," she admitted, referring to my mother's parents. "I'm sorry I didn't tell you. I truly didn't feel like it was my place," she reiterated. "I also was trying to keep my word to my dying best friend. I hope you understand. More than anything, I hope you understand my intentions weren't ill here."

Nodding, I let out a sigh. I was at a loss for words, though. I had forgiveness in my heart for Margot and Leo, because at the end of the day, Margot was right. It wasn't their secret to tell—it was my mother's, and she chose not to tell me. Instead, she didn't take her secret to the grave; she told two people, neither of which was me. Somehow, I needed to find forgiveness in my heart for her, too.

"Thank you for telling me now, Margot. I know it would be irrational of me to stay mad at you, because I agree with you. The person who should have told me the truth was my mother. I forgive you," I offered her.

I saw a glint from a fallen tear on her face as she walked around the checkout counter, squeezing me into a hug. I stood there for a moment before embracing it.

Still in the hug, Margot said just above a whisper, "Thank you, Jules." Pulling out of the hug, her hands on each of my shoulders, she gazed into my eyes and said, "Now about my son..."

"One thing at a time, Margot." I smiled.

"Understood." She smiled back.

twenty-six

$\mathcal{I}$ *was heading* back to Boston in a week and needed to confirm with my executive editor that I would be back at work soon. I sent her an email that I was indeed reporting back the Monday following my return to Boston—so in two weeks. She was thrilled to hear from me and said she "can't wait to have me back."

Being in Paris was a nice break from reality, but I was ready to get back to my normal life, especially back to work, too. First things first, I needed to call Gen to fill her in on the shitshow of events that had occurred and that I was heading back home soon.

"Doll, where have you been?!" she asked after one ring.

"Gen...I have so much to tell you," I trailed off.

"Spill it."

I told her everything that had happened with Leo and Margot, that I would be back to Boston and the magazine soon, and that I still had to decide how to leave things with Pierre.

"Let me ask you this," she began. "Do you love him?"

This was a question I undoubtedly knew the answer to. "I do, like I've never loved someone before. But it's just not that simple, Gen."

"Why the hell not?" she asked bluntly. I could see her face in my mind vividly: eyebrows raised, mouth twisted to one side, waiting for me to answer.

"Umm...because Boston is more than 3,000 miles from Paris. It would just never work. That's not a relationship, and you know it, Gen,"

"Have you ever wondered if he would consider moving to the States? I mean, Jules, he works for one of the biggest book publishers in the *world*. You don't think he could easily get another publishing house job...basically anywhere?"

She had a point. However, Pierre and I had known each other for only a few months, so that was a thought that had never crossed my mind—until now. Leave it to Gen to come up with a solution.

"You make a good point, but I just can't ask him to uproot his life for me. His mother is here, and this place...Paris, is all he knows," I admitted, but the wheels were still turning in my head, wondering if that was something Pierre had considered.

"I'm just saying it's something to think about. You never know, maybe that was something he considered." And with that, I knew Pierre and I needed to talk as soon as possible.

"Yes it is." I paused, biting my lower lip as I thought. "Hey, I need to go do something, but I'm so excited to get back and see you. Love you!"

"Likewise, Doll. Good luck with Pierre, can't wait to hear how it goes. Love you, too!"

We hung up the phone, and then the wheels in my mind were endlessly turning. The moment was here: *do I ask Pierre to come to Boston?*

My gaze flicked to a pile of photos I had gotten printed, photos Pierre had taken and some we had taken of the two of us. Picking up the pile of photos, I flipped through them. There was the one Pierre had taken of me with the Eiffel Tower behind me when we went sightseeing, a selfie we had taken on our hike, and a few from Loire Valley, including the one he took of me there with the peony he strategically placed behind my ear. I...we looked *happy*. Despite everything else, the undeniable joy leaking from our smiling faces when we were together was clear as day.

At that moment, I chose to love him for all the things he had done right and forgive him for the one thing he had done wrong.

Setting the photos down, I immediately dialed Pierre's number.

Pierre came over to the chalet so we could talk. It had been a week since I saw him last—at the Pont des Arts bridge when he told me Leo is my father. He respectfully obliged when I told him I needed some space. But now, here we were, facing the next big challenge.

"Jules, it's so good to see you," he said, giving me a tight hug and kissing the top of my head, while I slightly hesitated to fully embrace him.

Even though I had chosen to forgive him internally, there was still a pang of anxiety inside of me from when we last saw each other.

I closed my eyes, lingering in the moment, tears forcing a sting at the back of my eyes, because I didn't know how to say goodbye to him. I didn't want to have to. I wanted him to come to Boston.

"I've missed you," he said, patting my hair down.

Pulling out of the hug, staring into his beautiful gray eyes that mustered all the courage I needed to ask him to stay, I said, "I've missed you, too." I planted my lips to his, and I lost track of time, of where I was, of what we needed to talk about, for just a moment longer. Then, I pulled away as the intensity of why I was here grew bigger inside of me.

"So, my mother told me you two...sorted things out," he said matter-of-factly.

Offering a small smile, I said, "I guess you can say that. But, I asked you to come over because we need to...talk...about us."

He offered a small smile in return that resembled anything but happiness. "That we do."

We took a seat on the sofa. I sat cross-legged facing him, squeezing a pillow in my arms for a little bit of comfort.

"I think we know where this is headed," I said bluntly as I pinched the corners of the pillow. He nodded before I continued, "My departure from Paris is just days away now, and I mean it wholeheartedly when I say this is one of the hardest things I've ever had to do." A few tears escaped my eyes, and Pierre swiped them off my face with his thumbs.

"Jules, this doesn't have to be goodbye—" he started, before I cut in.

"Pierre, I love you. I love you so much it hurts. It hurts leaving you thousands of miles away. But we would both be fooling ourselves if we think this could ever work with that much distance." My words caused a pained expression to flash over his usually lit up features. "That's why I want to...ask you...do you want to come to Boston...with me?"

His face lit up, eyes twinkling, his lips turning into one corner of his mouth, but my words hung painfully in the air as I waited for his response. He looked surprised and happy that I asked, but I had no idea if he would take me up on the offer or not.

"Jules...I...I don't know what to sa—" he started, finally breaking the eternal silence.

"Say yes, Pierre," I cut in with a strained voice. It was my turn to set the rules now, to truly fight for what I wanted, and right now, he was all I wanted.

Taking a deep breath, he slowly crushed my spirit. "Jules, I love you, too," he professed, cupping either side of my face. "I wish more than anything that I could come with you, but my life is here...in Paris."

He squinted through teary eyes as all the color I had when he arrived drained from my face. "Pierre...I know you have an entire life outside of this little bubble we have created. But this...this can't be the end of us," I pleaded, struggling to find any more words. My heart dropped, and he was sticking his hand in my chest to pull it out slowly.

"Jules, believe me, this is hard for me, too, but—"

I interrupted him again, "Hard for you?" I could feel my sadness and pain turning into anger again, bile rising from my stomach to my throat. "My mother DIED. Then, I found out she lied about my ENTIRE existence. Then, I meet the man of my dreams that doesn't love me enough to actually take a leap and be with me?" I left my last comment open-ended, hoping he would take back what he said and just come with me.

"Jules..." the inflection in his voice dropped down to a somber tone, and I realized he wasn't going to change his mind. This was it.

I held up a hand to stop him from finishing his thought, because at that moment, despite Gen's thoughts on the situation, I couldn't bring myself to push him further to leave all he's ever known for me.

I cupped my hands over my face and released heavy sobs.

Pierre tried to console me, "Jules...come here," he said, trying to pull me closer to him, but I shook him off.

"D...don't," I said through my muffled voice. I paused for a moment, as if I was trying to calm down enough to finalize this conversation. "So, this is really it then, huh?"

"Yea, I think it is," he said, our gazes ever-present on each other.

I didn't know how to say goodbye to him. All I knew was I now had to. We had to. "I'm going to miss you so much."

"Come here," he said, pulling me into his chest as my sobs returned.

As he held me, I felt his tears dripping down my ears onto my face as my head was folded deeper into his chest.

In Paris, my heart was healed and broken all the same. I was leaving somehow with more clarity yet with more heartbreak. How do you say goodbye to the only man you've ever loved? I didn't know, but I knew I had to let him go.

Now, I needed to pack up my things, like I needed to pack up this short chapter of my life.

november

Dear Juliette | **Krys Marino**

twenty-seven

It had all started with a letter and led to the greatest adventure of my life. Who knew that the words *Dear Juliette* from my mother would mean so much and leave so much for me to figure out on my own. *I know you'll figure out what to do with what is left.* But she trusted I would find my way and be able to navigate a life without her. And yet, here I was just trying to survive my own mind—I still am.

Now that I'm back in Boston, I struggled with the notion of whether or not to contact Leo. After my experience in Paris, I felt like I closed the wound that was my mother only to realize there was one still open—I still didn't know what the future looked like with my father, with Leo.

If I were to stay even one more day in Paris, I would have overstayed my welcome. My time there was magical and provided closure I didn't know I was going to need. I fell in love with the city—and in the city, something else I hadn't expected when I stepped on the plane from Boston to Paris just a few months ago to put my mother to rest.

I never got to say goodbye to her before she had died, but now I realize she left this earth the way she wanted to—me keeping physical sight of the best of her and not seeing the disappointment, the devastation her secret caused me. She felt well-loved through the end of her life, and that's all that ended up mattering to me. Now that I knew the truth, I found myself forgiving all involved. That was my way of closing this chapter, leaving it behind in Paris, so I could embrace the future that lies ahead of me in Boston.

I ended up at the Boston Seaport, where I often came to think and just breathe while looking onward to the water. It was soothing. I seemed to have forgotten how brisk the air could be, even though the first fall of snow hadn't happened here yet, surprisingly.

I walked along the cobblestone lining the water, taking note of the dichotomy between how I felt walking this one versus the one in Paris. I never thought I would feel lost walking here as I did when I first arrived on the cobblestone road outside of my mother's chalet.

The last three months have shown me how to grieve, how to cope, and how to *love* unconditionally—even when you don't know how or where to start. I learned how to grieve my mother and cope with her death in my own way—by focusing on the love I had to give, by falling in love with Pierre. I learned how to love without condition—by forgiving my mother, Margot, Leo, and even Pierre for his little white lie. At the end of the day, love overshadowed the darkness in my life—it won.

Pierre was the first man I loved, because I never let anyone get close to me enough to love me like he did...does, other than Gen and my mother. All the other men I had flings with didn't earn a spot in my heart, in my life. They took and took, and all Pierre ever did was give...and give. They were verbally abusive; Pierre is kindhearted with his words. They pushed me to have sex on first dates; Pierre wouldn't even kiss me on the first date.

Not only did I have reasons not to trust men from experience, but I also realized I was holding onto a piece of my father that blocked something within me, shutting off my ability to trust them—to love them. He was the only man to see past that and stand by my side, as I searched for the answers of who my father is. The other men I thought were "nice" to me at the least were never patient enough to *understand* why I didn't trust them, even though they didn't give me reasons not to.

I already missed Pierre and mulled over our last conversation over and over again. He had become my new familiar, and although I was glad to be back in Boston and get back to work on Monday, reuniting with my best friend who I had missed dearly, my heart longed for him. I wondered if it would always long for him.

I pulled my phone out of my puffer jacket, holding it in my mittened palm. The time read: 2:39 p.m., which meant it was 8:39 p.m. Paris time. I pulled the mitten warming my right hand off and flipped through my call history until I found Pierre's contact. Before I clicked on it, an incoming call from an unknown number popped up on my screen. I was apprehensive about answering from an unknown number on my personal phone, which was nothing unusual, so I double-clicked the side button to ignore it.

A notification for a voicemail popped up twenty seconds later. I tapped on the voicemail, and my next step had been decided for me. It was from Leo.

Hi, Jules. It's...it's Leo. I just wanted to let you know I'm back in Boston and figured you would be back by now also. I don't want to force anything, and I know we can't rewrite the past, but I'd really love to get to know you. Let me know if you'd like to grab coffee sometime. Hopefully we can talk soon. Take care.

My heart was beating faster, although time felt like it stood still. After finding out Leo is my father, I wasn't sure what I wanted to do with that information. But now after hearing the effort Leo wanted to put in, to have me be part of his life, I left like we owed it to ourselves to try.

I locked my phone, sliding it back into the pocket of my jacket and slipping my mitten back on. I stuffed both of my hands into either side of my jacket as I watched the cold fog swirl off the water, and a few Great Black-backed Gulls were making khow calls to each other—two adults and one that appeared to be a baby trailing behind. To me, that was a metaphor, a sign. Almost like the two adult birds were threatened by me, trying to protect its baby. Maybe Leo trying to have a relationship with me after all these years of not knowing I was his daughter was his way of protecting me by no longer allowing me to live without a father.

"Hi, Doll, how was your walk?" Gen asked as I walked into our apartment. She was snuggled up on the couch in front of the TV with a cozy blanket and cup of hot chocolate. With her curly, natural hair pulled up into a messy bun and her bronzed skin free of makeup, she looked exactly the same as when I saw her last.

"A little chilly, but it was peaceful as always." I offered a small smile, taking off my jacket, boots, and mittens.

I left my boots by the front door, tossing my jacket and mittens on one of the island counter stools.

She narrowed her dark eyes on me. "Okay, what's up?"

Making my own cup of hot chocolate, I asked, "What do you mean?"

"Jules, we've known each other for years. I know when something is wrong with you," she pointed out before continuing. "I know a lot happened in Paris, and I know it's going to be an adjustment getting back to your normal life after all that but please don't shut me out. I'm here for you, and you know that. I've gone three months without having you here, so I really want you here with me...physically, mentally, emotionally."

Gen had a point. I have been back in Boston for almost a week now, and I have been completely checked out. From everything that went down with my mother, with Margot, with Leo...with Pierre. There were so many moving parts, so many changes, and it was going to be an adjustment getting back in the swing of things at work, at my *normal* life and routine. I hadn't heard from Pierre, either, and I think that was shaking me to my core—that things really were over between us.

My back was turned to Gen, and I took a deep breath before responding, "Leo left me a voicemail. He wants to...meet for coffee."

I finished making my cup of hot cocoa and turned around to see Gen with wide eyes and mouth slightly gaped. I walked over to the couch, sitting next to her as I waited for her response.

"W–Wow," was all she managed to say. Then after a brief pause, she asked, "Soo...what are you going to do?"

Holding my cup of cocoa in one hand and rubbing my forehead with the other, I admitted, "I'm going to call him back and tell him I would also like to meet up with him for coffee."

Her eyes were still wide as she blinked at me rapidly, pursing her lips, as if she was surprised by my response. "I can't say I'm disappointed. Quite the opposite, actually. I guess I'm just kinda surprised you would let him in so easily," she said bluntly.

Cupping my mug, I paused for a moment while her words sunk in. "I–I know." I struggled to find the words to explain. "But if I'm going to move on with my life, I need to forgive. Like really forgive. And although he knew I was his daughter when we first met, it's not like he knew my entire life." I briefly looked down at the untouched chocolate liquid. Looking back at Gen, I continued. "I think we should look at it like a fresh start, a clean slate. After all, it wasn't his fault my mother lied about him being my father, and he is now willing to make an effort to be in my life. How can I deny him that?"

Nodding, she said, "I'm proud of you, Jules. I know that wasn't an easy decision to make, but the fact that you came to it with such maturity shows how much you've grown. Damn, what's in the water over there in Paris?"

Letting a small laugh escape me, I said, "Touché. And thank you, Gen. That really means a lot."

Leo and I met for coffee at a little café on Boylston Street in Back Bay. When I walked into the café, my heart was pounding. Although I have decided to forgive Leo, I knew this interaction wasn't going to be easy—for either one of us.

He was already sitting at a table, waving me over. It reminded me of our meeting just a few weeks prior when I confronted him about being my father. The difference a few weeks—a few months—can make in someone's life.

I took my time walking over to him, trying to delay the inevitable. When I finally made it to the table, he offered a small and crooked smile and stood. He attempted to pull me into a hug, but after I showed hesitation, he seemed to have gotten the hint by offering a hand instead. "Jules, so good to see you."

Shaking it, all I managed to say was, "Likewise."

He sat back down, and I cautiously took the seat across from him.

We stared at each other for a moment before he broke the deafening silence. "So...how's it been being back in Boston so far?

Have you started back at work yet?" he asked, engaging in typical small talk, but I was thankful he started the talking.

"It's been okay. Quite an adjustment after...everything. But no, I go back to work tomorrow," I offered, my pounding heart starting to subside...just a little. The waitress came over and took our order. We both ordered black coffees, which was unusual for me, but I wanted to keep it simple—much like this conversation and meeting. "How about you? How have you been faring?"

His blue eyes were lighter, and his demeanor seemed lighter, too. Like a weight had been lifted from his shoulders. "I can't say I have any complaints." An awkward silence lingered in the air as it seemed we were both anticipating what to say, or do, next.

Thankfully, the waitress brought over our coffees. "Here you go, you two. Can I get you anything else?"

We both looked at each other before looking back at her and said, "No, thank you."

Nodding and smiling, the waitress said, "Very well. Let me know if you change your mind. Enjoy your coffee." She walked away, and we were forced again to interact with each other.

I mustered up the courage to continue the conversation. I figured now was as good a time as any to learn a little more about...*my father.* "May I ask, what exactly is it that you do?"

His smile grew bigger. "I'm a financial analyst for a private investment firm. I also handle international accounts, mostly in Europe, which is why I was in Paris..." he trailed off. He looked down at his coffee before returning his eyes to me. "How about you, do you like being a journalist?"

"How did you—"

"Your mother told me," he cut in.

Nodding, I answered him, "I love it. I'm a food writer."

A small laugh escaped him. "I can't say I'm surprised. Your mother definitely rubbed off on you in that sense. As soon as I found out about what you did from your mother, I took it upon myself to look up your articles. They are impressive, Jules. I can really tell you have a passion for what you do."

My mouth fell open at his disclosure. Leo clearly had taken an interest in me before I even knew about him. I felt how one would feel losing their keys and then finally finding them. "Leo...I–I don't know what to say."

"Do you want to start over?" he asked directly, his mouth in a straight line, eyebrows raised and looking at me intently.

I had forgiven him, and I felt like this would be the next step, but I was still hesitant. I didn't want us jumping into something neither one of us were ready for. Letting out a sigh, I pressed, "What exactly does that look like for us?"

"Well, for starters, like this," he suggested, holding out his hand in between us. "We have maybe a coffee date once or twice a week and go from there. Jules, I'm not asking for us to just act like nothing happened, like I didn't miss twenty-seven years of your life, but I am asking for you to try. I do want a relationship with you any way I can get one."

His admission caused tears to well in my eyes. I tried my best to hold them at bay as I composed myself for what to say next. He patiently gave me all the time I needed to give him an answer. After what felt like an eternity, I finally managed to say, "Okay...le–let's give it a shot."

I came here to forgive him, to see what could become of this—him and me—and I saw a light at the end of the tunnel. So, with everything I had, I accepted his offer. But not for him, for me.

We continued learning more about each other over the next hour: was he married? He wasn't. Did he have other kids? He didn't. Did I want to get married and have kids? Someday.

Our laughter filled the air, and it felt like a normal father-daughter coffee date just catching up, like no time had passed, like we didn't just spend twenty-seven years without being in each other's lives. I wondered if this is what it's like, hanging out with your father—awkward but silly, extraordinary and comforting at the same time. As the minutes ticked by, I felt the tension I came here with slowly lifting, and I could tell it was for him, too.

Fate sometimes has a funny way of bringing people together, and at this moment, I experienced wholly what that meant. Leo and I might never have a traditional father-daughter story, but maybe we were creating our own right before our eyes.

twenty-eight

My first day back at work was overwhelming. After being out of pocket for three months, I realized my beat had slipped a little bit after all the stories were handled among freelance writers. There was a lot of catch-up to do and assignments already lined up for me. But, after being in an international food center the last few months, I could confidently say I was stepping back into food writing with a more rounded perspective and refined palate.

I was wrapping up for the day and took the elevator down to the lobby. I didn't get good cell reception in the elevator, but when the doors opened, I saw I had a missed call—from Pierre. It was five-thirty p.m. here, meaning it was eleven-thirty p.m. Paris time. Why was he calling me so late?

Eager to hear from him, I quickly called him back. My heart was thumping abruptly against my ribcage at the sound of his voice. "Hi, Jules." My heart skipped a beat, and I wondered if I was still breathing. "Jules, you there?"

"Ye–yeah, I'm here. Pierre, is everything alright?" I inquired, my body instantly freezing in place hearing his voice for the first time in weeks.

"Haven't been better, actually," he said, leaving me to decipher what he meant by that.

"Is that so?" I asked rhetorically. "Want to enlighten me by what you mean and why you're calling so late?

"Look to the right of the lobby door," he said.

Doing as he asked, I saw a tall, handsome Frenchman holding a phone to his ear, wearing my favorite ear-to-ear grin on his flawless face—and carrying a bouquet of pink and red peonies.

"You...you're—" my breath hitched in my throat, threatening my ability to speak.

"Yes, I'm here, Jules."

Hanging up and dropping my phone into my bag, I half-sprinted up to him, throwing my arms around his neck and hugging him tightly. I instantly felt like my broken world had pieced back together. I was whole again.

Pulling away, I held his head in my hands, as if I were trying to make sense of him being here, trying to figure out if this was real.

"Oh my God, Pierre, what are you doing here?!" I shrieked, still in disbelief.

"Well, this is my new building," he said, opening his palm and looking around. "It's a nice one, I must say." He smirked, making my heart fall into my pelvis.

"Your new building?" I asked with furrowed brows.

"You know Hachette has an office...in this building, right?" he asked rhetorically, that cheesy smile with prominent dimples still plastered to his face.

"Well, yes, of course I do—" As I was saying this, it hit me. "Wait, you...you moved to Boston...to work at Hachette...here?" I asked, pointing to the ground, in even more disbelief, with excitement coursing through my body.

"Yes, Jules, I'm here to stay." He smiled with his eyes and lips, I so badly wanted to devour.

I couldn't comprehend what he was saying; his words weren't fully sinking in, but at the same time, I understood every word. Pierre moved to Boston, for me? After all was said and done, he chose me...again.

Without saying anymore words, I stood on my tiptoes and pressed my lips to his. I raked my sweaty fingers through his beautifully disheveled hair, as he kissed me back with everything he had, pushing my waist into his frame with one hand, as his other arm that was holding the peonies was snaked around my back. Anything and anyone around me was silent, as I soaked in every movement of his lips and breath on mine.

"Oww owww," I heard Gen call out from behind me, breaking up our reunion.

Giggling, I turned around, watching her as she smiled with her tongue sticking out and jumping up and down. She must have filed out of the office right after me.

Putting my hand on my hip, I said, "Yea...so that's my best friend Gen." I turned to face Pierre again, and we both just laughed.

Staring into those stormy gray eyes that looked as if they were longing for me, he looked down at the bouquet of flowers he was holding and said, "Oh, these are for you." He flashed his dimples again, holding out the flowers to me, and my world stopped. I would never get tired of these small but meaningful gestures from him.

Taking the flowers, I grinned back. "Thank you. They're beautiful." I briefly turned around to look at Gen again, and she quickly turned her head away like she wasn't staring at us. However, she stayed put and let us have our moment. I focused my attention back to the love of my life standing before me. "I've missed you...so much."

"I've missed you, too, love," he said, cupping my face between his hands and pecking my lips once more.

"So...real talk for a moment," I began, wanting to know what made him change his mind. "Why'd you decide to come here? I just thought when we last talked...well, you said your life was in Paris."

While one of my hands held the flowers, he lightly grabbed the other one while he looked at me intently, burning second irises in my eyes. "Shortly after you left, I realized my life is now here...with you, Jules. I want to start my life with *you*. Whatever it took, whatever that looks like now."

Tears stung the back of my eyes at his confession, and my words were stuck in my throat momentarily. "So, what's next?" I finally managed.

Wiping the tear threatening the corner of my eye, he asked, "How about dinner?" That grin I loved so much, the one that elevated his beautiful dimples, fell into place on his face, causing me to melt into his embrace. I swear any word to come from his French mouth—even if it was "poop," would have me swooning.

Holding the flowers behind my back, rocking back and forth on the balls of my feet, I humbly accepted his invitation. "Dinner it is," I said, biting my lip.

Holding my face in his hands again, he asked, "You know what?" He gleamed, like I was all he saw.

"What's that?" I answered, just above a whisper.

"I love you to the stars and back." I looked at him skeptically, squinting as my lips curled up into a smile, confident he got this well-known American saying all wrong.

"Don't you mean to the moon and back?" I countered.

His mouth broke into an all-teeth smile, so big that I was sure he couldn't have smiled any bigger. "Nope, the stars are farther."

epilogue

One year later

It has been one year since I returned to Boston from Paris. So much has changed since then, and I was living a life I didn't know was possible.

One year ago, I was lost. All of a sudden I was forced to live a life without my mother, the only home I had ever known, leaving the only person left for me, Gen. Now, one year later, I have not one beautiful man in my life but two—Pierre and Leo.

I wondered if I had never chosen to stay in Paris how different my life would look now. They say everything happens for a reason, and life is a series of choices that have been strung together to create your fate. I truly believed that.

Pierre had asked me to meet him at the Boston Seaport because he had yet another surprise for me. This man was full of surprises and never stopped short of amazing me.

Snow started to fall, so there weren't many people out at the harbor, leaving it peaceful and secluded, although very frigid. As soon as I laid eyes on Pierre though, his warmth radiated, making me forget how cold I was.

"Hi babe," I said, jumping into his arms.

"Hi darling," he said, smiling and planting a firm kiss on my lips. I loved kissing this man; it never got old. It always felt like two magnets were pushing us toward each other.

"So...what are we doing out here? You know it's November in Boston, wintry weather," I said, holding my hands out as fluffy, white snow laid specks on my gloves.

"I do know, however, this couldn't wait, and I know this is your favorite place." His wildly gray eyes bored into mine, as his lips turned up at the corners, making those dimples I loved so much appear. He lowered down on one knee and pulled out a small Tiffany Blue Box from his coat pocket. With a gasp, I covered my gloved hands over my mouth as he held out his hand and said, "May I?" I placed my left hand in his as he began to gently pull my glove off. "Jules, I knew from the moment I saw you on the Pont des Arts bridge that you were special. You may have thought distance was going to break us, but I wasn't going to allow that to stop me from being with the love of my life. Since then, you have made me the happiest man alive, and I can't think of a better next step than to ask you to be my wife. Will you marry me?"

Without hesitation I answered the most important question of my life, "Oh my God, YES, Pierre. Of course I will!"

I pulled him up to his feet, threw my arms around him, kissing him with everything I had. When we pulled away, he took the engagement ring from its box and slipped a round brilliant platinum ring with a halo of smaller diamonds lining the center stone onto my finger. It was perfect for me.

Gen materialized out of nowhere, wrapping her arms around me. As I turned to face her, squeezing her tight, Leo and Margot were trailing behind Gen. "Congratulations, doll! I'm so SO happy for you!"

"Thank you! I love you! Did you know?!" I asked her.

"Uh, duh. Of course I did. Who did you think helped this one pick out the most perfect ring for you?" She asked rhetorically, nudging Pierre in the arm.

"Fair enough." I gleamed, kissing her on the cheek.

I acknowledged Margot as she approached, opening her arms to hug me and congratulate us. She had visited for a week once over the last year, and although it was awkward at first, I knew I had to fully let go of the past in order to see my future. So that's what I did. And now she is my soon-to-be mother-in-law, and I wouldn't have it any other way. She still reminded me so much of my mother, as if she was carrying her spirit with her.

After embracing Margot, I reached for Leo to give him a hug, as he congratulated us as well.

Leo and I had grown closer over the last year. Our once-a-week coffee dates turned into weekly dinners until we were both naturally in each other's lives for all the moments you'd hope for in a father-daughter relationship. There would always be the past, but we agreed not to let that affect our futures.

After all was said and done, I was going to have someone walk me down the aisle after all.

The End.

acknowledgements

First and foremost, I want to thank my amazing support system in general—friends, family, and the Bookstagram community. I could not ask for a better group of people to cheer me on along the way of this wild and exciting journey.

For my Mom, you have always been supportive of my hopes and dreams, no matter how big or small. Thank you for being the shoulder I could lean on and the ear I could talk off when I needed it most. I love you.

For Dave, you aren't just the quintessential stepfather to me. You have always been there for me and for the family for the last fourteen years, and we are forever grateful for the love and support you've given throughout the years. I'll always love you as a daughter should love her father and appreciate our talks more than you know.

For my IMB family, I never thought when I started imPRESS Millennial I would have created the community of wonderful and talented women that it is now. We are partners, we are friends, we are a *team*. This publishing home would be nothing without each and every one of you. Together, we are making dreams come true and never forget your worth, especially what you mean to me.

For Harley, all the hell we've been through had a purpose—for the here and now. You are one beautiful, dorky soul, and I'm so happy to have found you. Thank you for inspiring the best parts of this book. I'd fall in love with you over and over again, and let you make me breakfast and iced coffees anytime. You'll always get the best of me.

For Monk girl, yes, I had to include my companion of fourteen years as one of the beings to be thankful for. She has been by my side as I wrote every word of each of my novels—the first one actually being about her. I thank her for making me laugh when I wanted to cry, for catching my tears when I did cry, and for loving me unconditionally. She will forever leave her *big* pawprints on my heart.

Last but not least, thank you to everyone who made it to the end of my second novel. Your readership means the world to me, and I hope you found a little piece of yourself in the struggles my main characters went through and know you aren't alone.

Printed in the USA
CPSIA information can be obtained
at www.ICGtesting.com
CBHW021706171023
1387CB00006B/78

9 781088 254387